OSCAR'S TALE

by

CHRIS BISHOP

HISTORIUM PRESS U.S.A.

In fond and loving memory of

'Lucky' Dave and Pip

With thanks for all the good years

A glossary of some of the terms as used

in this book can be found at the back

TABLE OF CONTENTS

Prelude	9
The Raid on My Father's Farmstead	11
We Seek the Sanctuary of Friends	19
I Begin the Quest to Find My Father	25
My Plea for Justice	32
The Eve of Our Departure	38
A Fool's Errand	45
I Learn the Harsh Realities of War	50
The Logistics of Battle	54
Our Plan for the Impending Battle	59
I Risk Trying to Free My Father	65
The Battle Unfolds	69
The Aftermath of Battle	74
Our Triumphant Return to the Vill	80
My Share of the Spoils	85
The Shadow of War Looms Over Us	90
The Prospect of Battle	94
We Prepare Our Defences	99
Cometh the Hour, Cometh the Foe	104
A Fatal Error	112
A Time and Place to Lick Our Wounds	116
We Go in Search of Our King	120
King Alfred's Return	126

We Prepare for Battle   133

The Battle of Edington   137

The Price of Peace   144

Glossary   157

Author's Notes   159

Acknowledgements   161

About the Author   162

'For is it not the wish of every man that

his son will achieve more in life than he did?'

PRELUDE

Ha, don't worry, I know what it is you want of me! You would know more about our great Saxon heroes who were so daring and bold that they feared nothing, not even death itself! That being so you'll not be disappointed, for my tale must needs include several battles - including the one near a place called Edington which must surely rate as one of the fiercest ever fought in this land. But first you must know how I came to be a warrior in the first place for, even as a child, I was given to bend my back to the plough rather than to wield a sword. Like other boys, I dreamt of battle fame and glory but, despite having once been a skilled and much respected warrior, my father refused to countenance me serving in the fyrd, saying that he hadn't reared me only to see me slain in the shield wall. Yet, as it transpired, the good Lord had other plans for me and, for reasons which I shall now relate, I was obliged to learn the ways of war even though I had then but fifteen years of age.

By the way, I was known then as Oscar, son of Oswald.

* * *

THE RAID ON MY FATHER'S FARMSTEAD

WESSEX – AUTUMN 877 A.D.

My story begins very early one morning when my father shook me till I woke. He then all but pulled me from my cot whilst urging me not to make so much as a sound.

'Get you to the woods,' he urged, his voice hushed and fearful. 'Take your sister and your mother with you then stay there. I'll come for you when I can!'

'Why? What's happening? 'I asked, still rubbing the sleep from my eyes.

'Raiders!' said my father. 'Seth and I will see them off but first I need you to get your mother and sister away from here.'

We lived in constant fear of raiders - men who came from across the sea seeking blood, booty or slaves. Some people called them "Danes" or "Norsemen", but we knew them to be Vikings – savage, cruel men who came from the distant lands in the north bringing death and destruction to our shores. Their lust for blood was such that they spared neither man, woman nor child and thus the very mention of them was enough to terrify me as it would anyone at that time.

'H…how many are they?' I managed to ask.

'I don't yet know. It's likely to be a small band of perhaps half a dozen which we should be able to deal with well enough - but I can't protect you all whilst doing so. Hence you must go now or they'll be upon us before we know it.'

My father was considerably older than my mother and had once served as part of the permanent guard at the Vill of Ealdorman AEthelred as a trained warrior. He oft times recounted tales of the battles in which he'd fought so I had no cause to doubt that he and old Seth, our farmhand, could defend our small farmstead well enough. As I prepared to do as he'd ordered, my mother was trying to comfort my little sister, Odelia, who was much distressed. Perhaps the fear felt by us all in that moment was infectious, although I doubt that she had any inkling of what was likely to befall us.

'Turn out the livestock as you leave,' insisted my father thinking quickly. 'If they've come for that they can round it up for themselves. Once you've done that, you know where to go, for I've shown you often enough.'

Of course, I knew the place well. It was a small clearing in the woods just beyond the field which formed part of our land - a place where we thought we would be safe enough. It was such that even if the raiders came looking for us, we'd see them coming and could move still deeper into the woods if we had to.

By then, even though Odelia was still crying, my mother had gathered up a few of our belongings and some food which she packed into a basket. Then, leading the way, I first did as my father had ordered and opened the stalls to the byre to let out our farm horse and our goats whilst my mother and sister drove both pigs from their sty and freed our few geese and chickens from their coop. That done, we hurried to the woods and from there to the small clearing where we hid as best we could, taking cover behind a thicket of scrub and thorn. I lay there on my belly peering out at the farmstead whilst my mother comforted Odelia, trying to keep her quiet lest the sound of her crying should carry on the cold early morning air.

From there I watched as my father and Seth came out from our home, both of them armed - my father with his sword and Seth with a short-handled axe which, although brutal, he had always professed to be his weapon of choice. As they waited for the raiders to show themselves, they stood back to back but kept far enough apart to avoid impeding each other's strokes.

At first there was nothing to be seen. Then, just as I began to think that perhaps the raiders had passed us by, men slowly emerged as if from nowhere, forming a ring around both my father and Seth and preparing to close upon them. I knew at once that all was far from well, for there were many more of them than the half dozen or so my father expected.

It was difficult to count the raiders from where I lay but I reckoned that they numbered at least twenty, possibly more. They were all on foot but seemed well armed with either a spear, axe or sword. Most of them had some sort of mail vest or at least a protective leather jerkin but, despite the cold, a few of them were stripped to the waist. However clad, they were all of them a terrifying sight to behold.

'God preserve us!' muttered my mother when she saw them. Even as she spoke, she started to pray, desperately whispering the words under her breath as she held Odelia in her arms and gently rocked her back and forth.

At first, the raiders just stood and stared at the men who confronted them, perhaps relishing what they thought would be an easy fight. The fact that my father was wielding a sword might have been reason enough for them to be wary as only trained warriors would be likely to own one but, given their numbers, they can hardly have expected much in the way of resistance from just two men. At that point, I also offered a silent prayer beseeching God to spare us. But God must have been busy elsewhere for, despite my pleadings, the raiders closed on my father and Seth with all the ferocity of wolves ravaging two all but defenceless lambs.

In fact, what happened next was so quick and so brutal that I can scarce bring myself even to describe it. What I recall was that Seth was the first to fall having being tackled by three men at once. In the struggle which followed he was struck by the flat edge of an axe so hard that it must surely have rendered him all but senseless. As he fell to the ground, they were upon him at once, beating him and kicking him so hard that I thought him killed for certain.

Even with Seth accounted for, my father continued to fight, hacking with his sword from side to side, forcing the raiders back. Even as he did so, others tried to take him from behind but he turned and, sweeping his blade in a wide arc, kept them all at bay. One of them risked ducking beneath his sword stroke but took a fearful wound for his trouble. As he staggered away nursing his shoulder, others quickly took his place. They then waited for my father to tire before grabbing him from behind and forcing him to the ground. I thought they would surely kill him there and then but that was not their intent. Instead, they struck him again and again until he was stunned and barely moving. Then, even as he recovered and tried to struggle to his feet once more, they quickly set about him again, three of them pinning him down whilst others bound his arms behind his back.

As they secured my father, Weasel, our wolfhound, went for one of the raiders, snarling and growling fiercely in such a way as I'd never known him do before. Without so much as a thought, the man turned and lashed out at him with an axe. I heard Weasel yelp then saw him slope off, whining and dragging his hind legs behind him. I cannot say how distressed I was to see him harmed in that way.

'No, Oscar!' pleaded my mother when she saw me drawing my sling from my belt. 'There's nothing to be done!'

I hesitated just long enough to see that she was right. After all, a sling would be useless against spears and axes. Besides, I realised that whatever I did would make no difference.

'Your father wanted us to stay together!' she urged. 'Besides, there's too many of them!'

I needed no reminder of what my father had said. Having seen enough killing to last him a lifetime, he had always been adamant that I should avoid fighting. 'Killing won't put food in our bellies,' he would say. 'Nor will it help our crops to grow.'

As I recalled those words I knew that my duty was to remain with my mother and sister. That being so, all I could do was watch as the raiders began to loot and ransack our home, seizing whatever they could find that looked to be of some use or value then either taking it, discarding it or destroying it as they saw fit.

One of them picked up my father's sword from the ground and examined it. Swords were much prized as a weapon, their value resting not so much on their worth in terms of silver, but on the reputation of the man who had wielded it - and on that of those whose blood had soiled its blade. My father's was a fine weapon which had once belonged to his father who had taken it in battle. It was therefore part of our family heritage and I was angry when I realised that the coward would take it for himself – something he could never have done in equal combat with such an accomplished warrior as my father, but there was nothing I could do to prevent it.

In the meantime, other raiders lit torches and began to set light to our home. They started by first burning our small cottage which, like others, was little more than a single room in which our family lived, ate and slept. With walls of timber and a roof thatched with straw, it was easy enough for them to set ablaze. They then raided our stores, stealing what little we had set aside for winter before torching the byre as well.

That done, they stood and watched for a while, cruelly jeering as our home burned. Then one of them noticed a small wooden horse on the ground, a toy which my father had made for me when I was younger. From that they knew that there were more of us living there so stood with their eyes scanning the woods where they guessed we would be hiding. Even so, they seemed ill inclined to come looking for us.

'They'll not come here,' my mother assured me, more in hope than in certainty. 'They believe the woods and forests to be the home of trolls and elves, not to mention all manner of evil spirits.'

I'd heard that said before but had to admit that those men didn't look as though they might be swayed by superstitious nonsense but, sure enough, it seemed they were done looting and started to prepare themselves to leave.

From what I could tell, my father had wounded several of their number, one of them so seriously that they callously shared out his rings and armbands between them. That done, they gave him his battle axe to hold and sat him up against a tree as best they could. It seemed strange to me that when too sorely wounded to be moved, they should leave him to die alone rather than put him out of his misery.

Finally, they pulled both my father and Seth to their feet even though both looked to be too shaken and unsteady to stand unaided.

At that they departed as silently as they'd come, forcibly dragging my father and Seth with them.

* * *

We couldn't remain hidden forever but waited long enough to at least be certain that the raiders wouldn't return before venturing back to what remained of our home. By the time we did there was nothing which could be salvaged. The flames had died down but most of the remaining timbers were blackened and still smouldering, some of them sending up showers of sparks as they collapsed into the still glowing embers. Looking around, the ground was strewn with our belongings, things they'd taken but then couldn't be bothered to carry with them so had discarded – not just pots and pans and such like, but also our personal things such as clothes and even tools. My mother fell to her knees when she saw all that and sobbed bitterly, desperately picking through the debris hoping to find something which hadn't been broken, spoiled or wasted.

I went first to examine the warrior they'd left behind. The only Viking I had ever seen close up before was a dead one who had been killed during a raid at a farmstead not so far from us, but this one, whilst fearfully wounded, was alive. He roared his defiance as I approached him but I could see that the wound to his upper arm had rendered him all but helpless.

He certainly looked to be fearsome enough with his face and arms painted with all manner of designs and his little black teeth filed into points. He was almost daring me to get closer, so I picked up a stout length of blackened timber and moved towards him. Even as I did so my mother called me back.

'Oscar, just leave him!' she scolded bitterly. 'He'll die of that wound soon enough. And more's the pity, for I would have him suffer for as long as it takes for what he and his kind have done to us.'

I knew she was right as the man's arm had been cut to the bone by my father's sword and was bleeding freely.

At that point I noticed Weasel's body which lay not far from there. It seemed he'd taken a cruel blow across his back and had crawled away to die, dragging his hind legs behind him and leaving a smear of blood on the ground as he did so. I couldn't bear to leave him like that so scooped him up in my arms and carried him to a spot behind what was left of our home and there buried him. I uttered a brief prayer for him but there was no time for anything more even though the sight of his mangled body upset me greatly. Although Weasel had been very much a working dog, my father always said that I'd spoiled him by treating him like a house pet. In a way that was true as it was me who had first named him for being as artful as a weasel – even when put out for the night you'd find him by the hearth in the morning and have no idea how he'd managed to get back inside! In fact, he and I had become inseparable having spent many nights together keeping watch over our few animals when we feared wolves were about.

'We can't stay here,' insisted my mother, sensing how upset I was. 'We have kin in the settlement at Fordingwic. We'll go there and get what help we can.'

'What about father?' asked Odelia.

'He's gone with those men,' explained my mother.

'But where has he gone?' pressed Odelia. Being much younger than me, she had never before seen the results of a raid at first hand although she must have heard others speak of the dreadful destruction which usually followed such brutal attacks. All I could do was look to my mother to answer her as best she could.

'We don't yet know,' she said coldly. 'But we'll find him, you'll see.' Even as she spoke she looked across at me, almost defying me to say anything more about what was likely to befall people who were taken by Viking raiders.

'Shall I first round up our livestock?' I offered changing the subject. 'The raiders didn't even bother to go looking for it.'

'No, others will help us with that. Let's be gone whilst we can lest the raiders' return, although God knows there's precious little left to interest them now – except perhaps ourselves as slaves.'

Of course, she was right. Our humble farmstead comprised of just a hide of land for which my father gave the Ealdorman a share of our produce in lieu of rent. Like all able-bodied men, he also served in the fyrd although, despite his military experience, he preferred to assist with civil duties such as mending the roads, ditches and defences rather than actually fighting. In between that, he worked all the hours he could to eke out a meagre living from the land which was mostly given over to crops to feed us plus a few goats and pigs and such like. Thus, with our home burned to the ground, our few belongings having been destroyed and with our livestock scattered, it seemed my mother was right, there was little left which would be of interest to anyone. The only thing of value left to us was our lives – and given the times in which we lived, even they weren't worth much.

WE SEEK THE SANCTUARY OF FRIENDS

We none of us spoke as we walked together towards Fordingwic, the settlement my mother had mentioned. As we went, I was thinking through all that which had happened and my mother was holding Odelia's hand, gripping it tightly to reassure her. To get there, we followed a rutted track for several miles until we reached a small cluster of buildings beside a shallow river crossing. Fordingwic had been established so that the people who lived there could offer their goods and services to travellers using an old Roman road which led eventually to Chippenham. At that time, there were several tradesmen there who had set up workshops, including a carpenter who utilised timber from the nearby forest and a potter who worked with clay from beside the river. There was also a mill a little further upstream where the water was deeper yet still flowed fast enough to turn a wheel for grinding corn.

We went to see my uncle Oswin who was the blacksmith in Fordingwic, knowing that he would help us if he could.

Emelda, Oswin's wife, came out to greet us as soon as she saw us arrive. She was a large lady with a kindly manner and seemed much concerned when my mother's courage gave way to a flood of tears as she explained what had happened. Emelda immediately ushered us inside her home and did what she could to console us.

Their home was much like our own except that it had a workshop at the back where Oswin plied his trade. 'He'll know what best to do,' she assured us and, with that, led us through to the smithy which, although open at the front, was still intensely hot from the forge and the air inside was thick with the smell of smoke and sweat.

Oswin was a big bear of a man who, because of the heat from the forge, worked stripped to the waist but wore a leather apron to protect himself from the sparks which were thrown up whilst hammering the heated metal. Strangely enough, whilst his stature was enough to convince others that he was not a man to be taken lightly, we all knew him to be a gentle giant.

As we entered, he was busy repairing a farm implement. He was so absorbed in his work that he barely even acknowledged us until he'd finished what he was doing. 'I'm sorry,' he said when he at last looked up. 'But once heated I must work the metal before it cools.' He then seemed to realise that something was wrong.

'Their farmstead has been raided,' explained Emelda, sparing my mother from having to speak of it again. 'They took both Oswald and old Seth with them then destroyed everything, even burning their home to the ground for no good cause.'

Oswin looked stunned by what she'd said. He and my father had always been close and it seemed that the news was almost too much for him to take in. He muttered something under his breath but it was clearly not something Odelia and I were supposed to hear. Then, as if to distract himself from that, he took a pair of tongs and used them to plunge the still red-hot metal he'd been working on into a pail of water to quench it. As the steam hissed and spat, he pulled the implement from the water and examined his handiwork. Satisfied with it, he laid it down on his bench then quickly glanced first at his wife and then at my mother. 'They'd be Vikings, then,' he said once he'd composed himself. 'I've heard tell of others in these parts who've been raided of late.'

To me, it didn't seem to matter much who the raiders were or where they'd come from; one band was as bad as any other. 'My father wounded one of them,' I boasted. 'They left him behind with his axe.'

'Aye, that's often the way of it,' said Oswin. 'See, they believe that if they die in battle they'll go to a place called Valhalla which is like heaven to them,' he explained. 'Their wounded will endure their pain for days in the hope that they can at least die fighting with whoever happens to find them.'

'So what's to be done with him?' I asked.

'I'll wait a day or so then go to finish him. After all, we wouldn't want him to die too quickly, now would we?'

We were all of us then silent for a few moments. 'But why do they come? And why do they have to destroy everything? Apart from my father and Seth, they took virtually nothing from us,' I reasoned.

Oswin put his hand on my shoulder. 'For them, taking a few slaves will be reward enough for their trouble,' he explained.

'Then why doesn't the King send men to stop them?' I asked, rather naively.

'Because a few raiders are not the worst of his troubles. An army of Vikings has already subdued all the Kingdoms north of here, including that of the East Saxons and both Mercia and Northumbria. He fears that they will soon turn their attention to Wessex and try to seize this land for themselves.'

I nodded as if to imply that I understood all that but, in truth, none of it made much sense. 'Then were the raiders part of that Viking army?' I asked.

'Probably not. Most likely they are just a band out for what they can get. They raid and pillage homes and farmsteads seemingly at will, taking slaves where they can and also stealing food with which to feed themselves. Whilst doing so, they look for other more profitable targets such as churches and the like.'

'Hence you should stay with us for now. Just until we can find you somewhere better,' suggested Emelda.

'Aye, that would be for the best,' agreed Oswin.

It was a very generous offer given that they had barely enough for themselves, never mind take on three more mouths to feed. Knowing that, my mother seemed inclined to refuse their hospitality, but Emelda wouldn't hear of it. 'And where else would you go in such times as these except to stay with kin?' she chided.

'We couldn't possibly…' tried my mother.

'I'll not hear of you going elsewhere,' insisted Oswin. 'You're more than welcome to share what little we have. Mind, it'll mean sleeping here in the smithy for now as we've precious little room as it is. But don't worry, we'll soon find somewhere for you to stay and at least you'll be warm and dry in here.'

As my mother thanked them both it seemed to me that everyone had forgotten the real issue. 'But what about my father?' I asked.

Oswin put his hand on my shoulder once more. 'Oscar, you do understand what will likely become of him?' he asked quietly. 'Having been taken alive, both your father and Seth will be sold in the slave markets abroad.'

I nodded as I needed no explanation about that, for I'd heard it said often enough that raids ended in one of only two ways – either all were slain or they were taken for slaves. What he didn't say was that without my father and Seth to rebuild our farmstead, we would surely lose our land if we couldn't pay our dues. 'So what can we do?' I pleaded.

He looked at me coldly. 'Nothing,' he said. 'I'm sorry, but that's the way of it.'

'But there must be something!' I protested.

'Well, you could report the attack at the Vill. You'd need to see Ealdorman AEthelred in person for that but he's a very busy and important man. Your only chance is that he'll deign to see you because he once knew your father when he served as a member of the Vill guard, although even then he'll need persuading to actually do something about it.'

'Will he not send men to get my father back?' I asked.

Oswin shook his head. 'I doubt it,' he said. 'He's none too keen on fighting raiders unless he has to. He'd rather leave them to depart of their own accord than risk the lives of even more men trying to stop them.'

Realising that my father might well be lost, I couldn't stop the tears from welling up in my eyes. 'But…'

'There is just one possibility,' continued Oswin on seeing how upset I was. 'Lord AEthelred is a very pious man and if he thinks the raiders intend to strike at a church or a monastery, he may well be inclined to act if only for the good of his soul. So, if you do get to see him, try to imply that might happen.'

'But how do I find him?' I asked.

'As like as not he'll be at his Vill by now. He usually spends the winter there. Do you know the way?'

I shook my head as I'd seldom travelled even as far as Fordingwic before, much less crossed the river.

'It's not so far from here,' Oswin assured me. 'Cross the ford then follow the river downstream. There's a narrow track between the river and the forest which will lead you to a much larger settlement than this one. You'll see the Vill plain enough when you get there.'

'Will you not come with me?' I asked.

Oswin shook his head. 'I would if I could but I've work enough to do here, particularly if we're to feed you all. Besides, he'll more likely take pity on you.'

I looked across to my mother.

'Don't go, son,' she pleaded. 'Remember that your father wanted us to stay together.'

'I know, mother, but if I could just persuade Ealdorman AEthelred to help us...'

'Oscar, I've already lost my husband, would you have me lose my son as well?' she said, close to tears once more.

'But mother, I have to save father if I can,' I reasoned. 'Without him we'll all starve. Besides, he'd expect me to at least try.'

She considered that then seemed to agree, albeit reluctantly. 'Very well,' she said. 'But only as far as the Vill, do you hear me? Not one step further. See Ealdorman AEthelred if you can and tell him what's happened, then come straight back here.'

'Yes mother.'

'If Oswin and Emelda will have us, Odelia and I will wait here for you to return.'

At that, she handed me her cloak as proof against the cold. As I tucked it under my arm meaning to put on it once outside, Oswin turned and picked up a knife which he'd been repairing. He tested the blade with his thumb and then, not satisfied that it was sharp enough, used a grinding stone to improve its edge before handing it to me.

It looked more like something for skinning hares rather than to use as a weapon. 'I wouldn't know how to use this if it came to a fight,' I said, feeling slightly ashamed to admit as much. 'As you know, my father was adamant that he wanted me to avoid fighting so never showed me how. I'd best rely on my sling.'

With that I showed him my sling, a simple affair which I'd made for myself. I also showed him the few carefully chosen pebbles I always carried in a pouch attached to my belt but I could see that he was hardly minded to regard the sling as a potential weapon.

'I've no doubt that serves you well enough when seeing off foxes or even wolves, but you'll need something more than that if you're obliged to defend yourself, so take the knife as well.'

I hesitated, still unsure as to whether I should accept it.

'Take it boy,' he urged. 'With luck you won't have cause to use it. But there's no telling who you'll meet on your journey and some of those you come across will be less worthy than the sort of men you're used to. Just tuck it into your belt so that it can be plainly seen, for few men will try you if they can see you're armed. Besides, they won't know whether you know how to use it or not.'

I BEGIN THE QUEST TO FIND MY FATHER

What concerned me about going to Lord AEthelred's Vill was not the distance I would need to travel nor the time it would take for me to get there - although I knew that I needed to make what haste I could. What worried me was the prospect of meeting men on the road who might seek to take advantage of a boy travelling alone. Sure enough, having gone some distance, I came upon a man who was idly waiting beside the track.

'So, what brings a young rascal like you to these parts,' he challenged, trying to sound more friendly than he appeared.

I stopped well short of where he loitered, fearful of what he had in mind given that he looked to be both dirty and brutish, with his face unshaven and his hair hanging lank and loose about his shoulders.

'What's the matter, boy?' he asked as he crossed to stand in front of me and, in so doing, blocked my path. 'Have you lost your tongue or have you nothing to say for yourself?'

I decided it was best not to answer that but instead did the worst thing possible by pulling out the knife Oswin had given me and holding it where the man could plainly see it. Even as I did so, I knew it was a mistake.

'So that's to be the way of it?' he sneered, then produced a blade of his own. His was a seaxe – a short bladed sword with a single edge, a weapon which was more than a match for my small knife. 'Don't be a fool!' he warned. 'Pulling that puny blade serves only to make me wonder what else you have which might be of interest to me.'

'I've got nothing for the likes of you!' I said, trying to sound braver than I felt.

'Ah, the likes of me, is it? And what would that be coming from a wretch like you?' He then looked me up and down for a few moments as if expecting me to run, but I knew better than to turn my back on a man when challenged. 'Look about you, boy,' he threatened, holding up the seaxe as if to make his point. 'This forest is a lonely place in which to die and that knife you have won't save you. Thus, unless you've something better with which to defend yourself, you'd best give me that cloak from your shoulders and maybe then I'll let you pass unhindered.'

I took him at his word and tucked the knife back into my belt but pulled out my sling instead. 'There is this,' I replied, hurriedly picking a stone from my pouch whilst still keeping my distance. 'So, if you want what's mine, you'd best come and try to take it.'

Being used to guarding our livestock against predators, I was well practised with the sling; so much so that he'd taken barely a few steps towards me before I spun it round above my head then loosed a stone with all the force I could manage. At such close range I found my mark easily enough and the stone struck him directly in one eye. He groaned and, clutching his head, turned away in pain. For a moment he seemed to steady himself but then dropped to his knees, one hand still covering his eye but with blood welling out from between his fingers. I hurriedly prepared to loose another stone but he held up his other hand as if imploring me not to strike him again.

I was tempted to take the seaxe which then lay on the ground between us but quickly decided against it as I had no idea how to wield it. Instead, I walked past him. 'You're lucky,' I told him as I did so. 'I could have easily killed you if I'd been so minded so perhaps you should take more care about who you try to rob. Next time I might not let you off so lightly and, as you said yourself, this is a very lonely place in which to die.'

* * *

For the rest of my journey I followed the river just as my uncle Oswin had advised, carefully keeping to the narrow path which ran very close to the muddy bank and was quite slippery and treacherous in places. It was certainly not a path which was much travelled so I realised that there was probably a better track to serve such an important settlement as one which included an Ealdorman's Vill, but I decided not to waste time trying to find it.

As I went, I hoped that my father would be proud of me for having stood my ground against the robber. Yet my thoughts were still tinged with remorse at having inflicted such a dreadful wound on the man; one which would almost certainly result in him being blinded in one eye. All I could think of to console myself was that he would have surely killed me soon enough had he prevailed.

* * *

It turned out that the settlement was not so far from there and I found it readily enough. It was a sprawling cluster of homes, sheds and stores which had all been built within the shadow of the Vill which was, itself, set slightly apart and enclosed by a tall timber stockade.

There was a footbridge across the river at that point which I used to reach the far bank, then made my way straight towards the Vill gates which it seemed were kept wide open. As I approached, two guards stepped out seemingly ill inclined to let me pass unchallenged.

'What business have you here, boy?' demanded one of them. They looked formidable enough and were both armed with a spear and a shield.

Given that I was a stranger there, I'd expected to be challenged so took no offence. 'Sir, our farmstead has been raided and my father has been taken for a slave,' I answered respectfully.

'So?' sneered the guard. 'And what the hell would you have us do about it?'

'I was told to come here in haste and to speak to Lord AEthelred in person,' I said.

'Ah! But does he want to speak with you boy? That's the question.'

I wasn't sure what he meant by that. 'But I need to find the raiders and rescue my father before he's taken abroad,' I explained.

'Well,' teased the other guard. 'If that's so, why waste your time coming here? Would it not be better to chase after them yourself? With that knife you have tucked in your belt I'm sure they'll quake with fear when they see you coming!'

They both laughed heartily at that.

Being questioned was one thing but I hadn't expected them to mock me. 'I came here seeking the Ealdorman's help, not to be treated like a fool,' I said defiantly.

'Did you now?' said the guard, surprised at my bold response. 'And why would Lord AEthelred want to help a wretch like you?'

'I don't know, but I've no time to waste having already been delayed by a rogue who was intent on robbing me.'

'Is that so? And what did you do about that?'

I hesitated before answering. 'Put it this way,' I said at last. 'Next time our paths cross I doubt he'll be quite so keen to confront me.'

The guard looked me up and down. 'Are you saying you took him on with just that knife?' he asked.

'No, I didn't need the knife once I'd all but taken out his eye with my sling!'

The guard was suddenly silent. 'Feisty little runt, aren't you?' he said, clearly impressed.

'Look, my father, Oswald, son of Ogbert once served in the guard here. He'll soon be taken abroad and, once that happens, I'll have no hope of freeing him.'

At that the other guard recognised my father's name. 'Oswald? Are you then his son?' he asked.

'I am,' I said proudly. 'Do you then remember my father?'

'Aye lad, that I do. Or at least, I remember a man of that name. If you say he's been taken then I'll wager that he proved more than a handful for a few cowardly raiders! Whilst serving here he was regarded as being a very brave and able warrior.'

I wasn't surprised to hear that, for my father had often spoken proudly of his time as one of the guards. 'That's true enough,' I said. 'Even though hopelessly outnumbered, he and our farmhand gave a good account of themselves. My uncle Oswin said they were probably Vikings who attacked us.'

'Pah! Vikings or Danes – call them what you will. They're all marauding heathens who have no business being here.' He then seemed to have further thoughts about my predicament. 'You'd best come through to the Hall. Even once there I can't promise that Lord AEthelred will see you but, if you're Oswald's son, Wulfric may be inclined to help you.'

'Who's Wulfric?' I asked.

'Wulfric is head of the guard here.'

'So why would he help me?'

'I'll let him explain that. Just follow me and don't speak to anyone unless you're spoken to, do you hear me?'

With that, he led the way through the gates and into the grounds of the Vill itself. As we went, we passed numerous outbuildings, including stables, kennels and even an aviary which contained two beautiful falcons. When we at last reached the main Hall, I found that it was surely the biggest building I'd ever seen, being built of strong vertical timbers under a thatched roof which sloped down almost to the ground. There was a large canopied porch over the entrance, the fascia and eaves of which had been intricately carved and brightly painted. Within the porch were two sturdy doors which were also guarded.

The guard who escorted me there spoke to one of those on duty and explained what I wanted. He was at first curious to know why a man like Wulfric would wish to even speak with the likes of me but, when the guard explained who I was, he went inside the Hall. He reappeared after several minutes to say that Wulfric would come to see me shortly and that I should wait. Even from what little had been said, I realised that Wulfric must be a very important man within the settlement, perhaps second only to the Ealdorman himself.

After what seemed like a very long time, a man appeared and looked me over. I noticed that he walked with a limp and had long black hair which was braided to show he was a warrior. In fact, everything about him suggested that he was a man to be reckoned with. 'I'm Wulfric,' he said. 'Head of the guard here. I gather you wish to report a raid?'

'That's so my Lord.'

'I'm not your Lord,' he said correcting me. 'It's best that you know the way of things from the outset. That honour belongs to Lord AEthelred alone who is Ealdorman here. As to whether he has time enough to speak with you is another matter.'

'Thank you, sir. Forgive me, for I have never addressed anyone of importance before.'

He smiled at that as if he found it amusing. 'The guard said you're Oswald's son and that your farmstead has been raided. Is that the way of it?' His tone was softer now, thereby showing that he was not as stern as he had at first appeared.

'It is, sir. And the raiders have taken my father for a slave.'

He seemed surprised at that. 'I'm right sorry to hear that. I knew your father when he served in the guard here and regarded him well. He was a good man so, for his sake, I'll see what I can do to help you.' With that he led me through the doors into a sort of lobby where he told me to remove any weapons. I dutifully placed not only my knife but also my sling on the table which caused Wulfric to smile wryly. 'Now boy, remember to kneel in front of Lord AEthelred unless he invites you to stand,' he advised, realising that I would know nothing of such courtesies. 'And speak only when you're spoken to and never turn your back on him, even when you leave. He'll take it as a slight if you do.'

I thanked him for the advice then waited whilst he went through to the main chamber. I knew it could well be sometime before I might be admitted as Wulfric had warned me that there were many men who were anxious to speak with the Ealdorman that day, all of them far more important than the likes of me.

MY PLEA FOR JUSTICE

When Wulfric eventually re-appeared he led me through to the inner sanctum of the Hall itself, a huge chamber with a vaulted ceiling and walls which were hung with various embroideries - some depicting scenes from the Bible and others which portrayed tales from our great Saxon heritage. It was warmed by a central hearth where a log fire burned brightly and lit by several tapers which smoked and flickered, casting shadows on the walls.

The Hall was crowded with people, some of them no doubt part of Ealdorman AEthelred's retinue of advisers who were all seated on either side of him, plus others who had found a place on one of the many benches or were standing at the back. Most were no doubt there seeking justice or were intending to plead their cause on some matter or other. Lord AEthelred himself was at the far end of the Hall, attended by his Reeve and seated on a beautifully carved chair which was mounted on a raised dais. I had never seen him nor his likeness before but he was much as I'd imagined – although was perhaps even older than I expected, with silver hair and cold grey eyes. He was busily construing a document so that he barely looked up even when Wulfric told me that it was at last my turn to approach him. As I did so, I moved slowly towards him with my head meekly bowed then dropped to one knee at what I felt would be a respectable distance. I had never before felt so nervous as I did that day and my heart was pounding in my chest as I waited for him to speak.

'So, who have we here?' he asked at last, briefly glancing up at me before returning his attention to what he was reading.

'My Lord, my name is Oscar, son of Oswald,' I replied.

He seemed then to ignore me before Wulfric spoke up for me.

'My Lord, you may recall this boy's father; Oswald is a freeman who holds land from you and once served here with distinction as a member of your guard.'

That seemed to prod his memory. 'Ah, I remember your father as will others here. You look so like him that I should have known you at once,' he said, still barely affording me more than a glance. 'Do you have his courage as well?'

'I hope so, my Lord. Although I doubt I could ever match his skill as a warrior.'

'Then do you not yet serve in the fyrd?' he pressed.

'No, my Lord. At least, not for military duties but I help to maintain the footways and ditches.'

He seemed satisfied with that. 'Good. Wulfric informs me that your farmstead was raided this morning and that your father was taken?'

'Quite so, my Lord. He was hopelessly outnumbered but prepared to make a fight of it. Unfortunately...'

He held up his hand to stop me saying more. 'I don't doubt any of that. And I'd have expected no less from your father for as I recall he was never one for holding back when it came to a fray! So, what would you have me do about it?'

'My Lord, would it not be possible to send men to free him?' I asked.

He seemed surprised at the request. 'And how the hell would you have me do that? he asked bluntly.

'Could you not intercept the raiders, my Lord?' I tried, somewhat weakly. 'They can't yet have got too far.'

'Well, we could,' he laughed. 'But how many were there in this raiding party?'

'At least twenty, my Lord. And there were perhaps others I couldn't see. They headed south after the raid so…'

Once again he didn't let me finish. 'If they were headed towards the coast then as like as not we're already too late,' he reasoned. 'It's a little more than a day's march from here and they'll have a longship tucked away somewhere so will have set sail long before we can reach them.'

That seemed to be his final word on the matter and he returned to reading the document, but I wasn't about to give up. 'My Lord, surely if we hurry…'

'Don't be a fool, boy,' he snapped, clearly not amused. 'We'd never muster enough men to match their numbers in time to intercept them.' With that he turned to Wulfric who, having shown me into the Hall, had waited whilst his Lord spoke to me. 'Is that not so, Wulfric?'

Wulfric stepped forward. 'My Lord, assuming we leave a contingent of men sufficient to protect the Vill whilst we're away, we could muster about a dozen men from here at best. We could, of course, raise the fyrd, but they'd be mostly farmers and tradesmen, so no match for a warband of battle-hardened Vikings.'

'They were all on foot, my Lord,' I tried desperately. 'And probably had other slaves as well who will doubtless do what they can to slow their progress.'

Lord AEthelred looked shocked that I should dare to press my point, but I continued nonetheless, recalling my uncle Oswin's advice. 'As they took so little of value from our farmstead, my Lord, will they not now look to take plunder from elsewhere before they leave our shores? Surely, even if they have enough slaves, are there not churches or monasteries they can raid on their way to the coast?'

It was Wulfric who spoke next, perhaps to cover for my having spoken out of turn. 'My Lord, as you'll recall, we have reports of other farmsteads being raided over the past few days. Slaves were taken there as well but little in the way of plunder.'

Lord AEthelred seemed to acknowledge what Wulfric had said. 'Three farmsteads in total as I have it,' he said grimly. 'But it's too late to put that to rights. These raiders strike fast and are then gone before we can stop them. We have no chance to intercept them unless we first have warning of their coming. That's just the way of it, boy.'

'But surely my Lord, we must do something to stop them? With my father taken and our farmstead destroyed, we'll not be able to pay you what's due from our harvest so…' I stopped there, realising that would be of only nominal concern to the likes of Lord AEthelred. He was, after all, both rich and powerful, being a distant cousin of no less than King Alfred himself. The loss of our modest contribution to his coffers would therefore be of little consequence to him.

'And for that you would have me go chasing after them? That being so, then all I can say is that you seem to understand very little of these matters. Therefore let me enlighten you. For one thing, to go chasing after them would mean dragging a lot of other men away from their work on the chance that we may catch up with these heathen bastards. For another, there would be a very real risk of incurring losses if we do manage to confront them. The death of several good men would only compound my loss.'

It was Wulfric who then spoke again. 'My Lord, there is another matter to consider. The Minster of St Matthew lies between here and the coast.'

Suddenly one of the men seated among those to one side of Lord AEthelred seemed to find that of particular interest. I later learned that he was called Bishop Leonfric.

'My Lord,' protested the good bishop struggling to his feet. 'That being so, I must urge you to take what action you may. The Minster of St Matthew has several holy relics which must be saved. Besides, there are many monks who serve and worship there, not to mention a priest and some laymen, all of whom warrant your protection.'

Suddenly Lord AEthelred was interested. Being a pious man, it was just as Oswin had suggested insofar as the prospect of a church or a monastery being raided was enough to persuade him to act. 'And you think they may seek to attack the Minster?' he asked, looking back at Wulfric.

Wulfric merely shrugged. 'It's certainly a possibility, my Lord. And if so, what young Oscar here has suggested may make sense after all,' he offered.

'So what's to be done?' demanded Lord AEthelred.

I realised then that Wulfric was not just head of the guard, he was also skilled in the ways of the court having let Bishop Leonfric press the case for him – and for me. 'I could send runners tonight to summon the fyrd and have them here by morning,' he suggested. 'We know the road to the coast well so, if we leave at first light and travel swiftly, we could possibly reach the Minster before the raiders. After all, as young Oscar has said, contending with the slaves they've already taken will slow them down.'

'And what then?' demanded Lord AEthelred.

'My Lord, a show of strength might at least persuade the Vikings to make straight for their ship instead. The monks might thereby be spared as would the Minster itself.'

I began to see that whatever action was taken would have little or nothing to do with freeing a few Saxon slaves whose lives seemed not to matter. It was more about protecting the interests of the Holy Church and thereby Lord AEthelred's soul.

'How many men would you need?' asked Lord AEthelred.

'My Lord, I would suggest just ten guards from here plus thirty members of the fyrd. I should also like to take Rufus as well if you can spare him for a few days.'

'Why would you need Rufus?' he queried, clearly not much liking that idea.

'My Lord, if we're too late and find they've already raided the Minster they'll likely return to their longship with their slaves and whatever plunder they've manged to accrue. If so, we'll have the devil's own job to find them.'

'And you think Rufus could help with that?'

'Indeed my Lord. He has tracking skills beyond those of any man I know.'

Lord AEthelred seemed to accept that. 'Very well,' he agreed. 'Take him with you if you must. But you keep him safe, do you hear me? He's the best hunter I've ever had and I'll not take it well if you return without him.'

'Of course, my Lord,' agreed Wulfric.

'And remember, you engage the raiders only if you're obliged to. There's no merit in risking the lives of our men just for the sake of a few who have already allowed themselves to be taken,' he said, looking directly at me.

'Thank you, my Lord,' I said. 'May I wait here until they return?'

'Wait here?' he stormed. 'Why in God's name would you wait here? You're to go with them! After all, it's your father they're trying to save so you must play your part as well. Is that not fair?'

'My Lord, I've never fought before,' I stammered, not expecting that.

'Pah! What age have you, boy?' he demanded.

'My Lord, I've known but fifteen summers,' I told him.

'Then it's time you learned! Does your mother know you're here?'

'She does my Lord.'

'Then it's settled,' he decided, then looked hard into my eyes. 'Stay close to Wulfric and do exactly as he tells you,' he warned. 'For I wouldn't want to explain to your poor mother that you've managed to get yourself killed, not with her husband having so recently been taken from her.'

THE EVE OF OUR DEPARTURE

'Can you ride, boy?' asked Wulfric as we walked past the stabling area.

'Yes,' I lied, but then quickly regretted it when I saw the horses he had in mind. They all looked to be half wild and barely trained to the saddle.

'Then you'll have to get used to them, and quickly so,' teased Wulfric when I confessed that the only horse I'd ever ridden was our old farm horse which I used to ride bareback whilst clinging to its mane! 'Don't worry, you'll not be riding tomorrow,' he then said to reassure me. 'We'll need to move fast if we're to reach the Minster in time, so you'd best travel in the cart which will be used to carry our baggage. Even so, you'll need to keep up; the men won't wait should you fall behind.'

'How many of us will there be?' I queried.

'Hopefully by the time the members of the fyrd arrive we'll number over forty if you include Rufus and myself.'

'Will that then be enough for us to take on the raiders?' I pressed.

He looked at me before he answered as if assessing the numbers for the first time.

'No, not if it comes to a straight fight,' he decided at last. 'What I have in mind is a show of strength which will hopefully suffice to deter them from attacking the Minster. That's assuming we get there in time.'

'So how then will we rescue my father?' I asked.

'I don't yet know,' he admitted. 'We'll need to see how things are when we get there but I'll not lie to you, there may be nothing we can do without risking the lives of others which would make no sense whatsoever. As a warrior, your father will understand that all too well. Now, what weapons do you have?'

I showed him the knife which my uncle Oswin had given me. He looked at it doubtfully before handing it back to me. 'Do you at least know how to use it?' he asked.

'Well enough,' I lied again. 'I also have my sling.'

He laughed when I mentioned that. 'Much good will that do you!' he said.

'It served me well enough earlier today when a man tried to rob me whilst on my way here,' I boasted.

'How so?' he asked.

'I all but took his eye out when he made to attack me with a seaxe.'

'Did you, by God! Then perhaps we'll make a warrior of you yet! But remember, whilst a sling is good for protecting your livestock, it won't help you much when confronting a blood crazed Viking warrior!'

I was not so sure about that; it seemed to me that a well-aimed stone from a sling would be deterrent enough for anyone, whether it be a Viking raider or a rogue trying to rob me but, in the end, I said nothing.

'Anyway,' continued Wulfric. 'We leave at first light so you need to be up and ready by then. You can sleep here tonight on one of the benches in the Hall. There'll be others there as well but I'd advise you to keep yourself to yourself. They'll mostly be members of the fyrd who can be very rough company once they set themselves to drinking.'

'Thank you,' I said.

He seemed surprised at that. 'What for? he asked.

'Without you and the good Bishop Leonfric, I don't think Lord AEthelred would have agreed to help me rescue my father,' I explained.

'Well, for my part I've reason enough for that; but this is not the time to speak of such matters as there's much I need to prepare for our mission tomorrow. Besides, like I said, there may be nothing we can do.'

'But surely they'll be enough of us to…'

He didn't let me finish. 'At least half our men will be farmers, not warriors, and we'll be fighting men whose lives are steeped in blood. They'll not think twice about killing any of us, you can be sure of that. What's more, anyone who's taken alive will soon wish he'd let himself be killed when he had the chance!'

'So what will happen if we don't rescue my father?' I asked, almost dreading the answer.

'Your father is a proud man so slavery will be even harder for him to endure than for most. As a Viking slave, he'll be half starved, regularly beaten and probably chained to a post when he isn't working. But that's not the worst of it. Few people know what it is to lose your freedom. It saps your strength to the point where you regard your life as no longer worth living.'

'So we must save him if we can,' I urged.

'Yes,' said Wulfric. 'But we can only do our best. Anything more than that is in God's hands - not mine nor even the mighty Lord AEthelred's.'

* * *

I was told to return to the Hall to sleep where I would also be given something to eat. Having done so, it seemed to me that the place was filled fit to burst given that the members of the Ealdorman's retinue were still there, not to mention those members of his guard who were not on duty elsewhere. Later it became even more crowded as members of the fyrd began to arrive as well. When it came to time for us to eat, the most important men were seated at a table with Lord AEthelred himself, all enjoying a lavish supper which included so much food that even half of what each of them consumed would have sufficed to feed our family for a week! The men of less obvious worth were seated where best they could find a vacant spot but were offered a more modest meal of boiled mutton and a cake of bread.

Once supper was over, I wandered outside to get some fresh air and noticed a young girl who was the prettiest I'd ever seen. Her hair was tied back and covered with a blue headscarf but, apart from that, she was dressed in a plain smock which was belted about her waist. I assumed she was one of the servants so went over to speak with her when I noticed she was looking at me.

'What's your name?' I asked, pleased for the chance of speaking to someone of about my own age.

She hesitated before answering. 'I'm called Edwina,' she said reluctantly.

'So, Edwina, do you work here?' I asked.

She laughed, then started to turn away.

'What's the matter?' I asked.

She laughed again. 'Nothing,' she said. 'It's just that I'm not permitted to speak to strangers.'

'I'm not a stranger,' I protested. 'I'm going with Wulfric and the others tomorrow to fight the raiders.' Even as I said it, I felt that it sounded rather boastful given that I would be barely tolerated on the mission and, as like as not, would make a fool of myself.

'I know who you are,' she informed me. 'You're the boy who has come to rescue his father.'

'That's right,' I acknowledged, surprised that she should know that.

'My father says that you're too bold for your own good.'

'Your father?' I queried.

'Yes, my father is Lord AEthelred who is the Ealdorman here. I gather you spoke with him earlier?'

At that I wasn't quite sure what to say. No wonder she didn't speak to strangers, much less people like me who were far below her station in life. 'I'm sorry, I didn't realise,' I tried somewhat pathetically. 'I didn't notice you at supper and...'

'My mother and I prefer to dine in her chamber when the fyrd have been summoned whereas my father likes to eat with his men. Anyway, I hope your mission succeeds,' she added, then turned and walked away. As I watched her leave she glanced back at me and smiled.

* * *

Later that evening, another man also came out for some fresh air and, upon seeing me, wandered across to speak with me. He introduced himself as Rufus.

'Are you then Lord AEthelred's hunter?' I asked, recognising the name from when I'd spoken to Lord AEthelred.

'Aye, that's me,' said Rufus. 'And you I take it are the bold young knave who insists on coming with us on this fool's errand tomorrow.'

I laughed nervously. 'Why is it a fool's errand?' I asked.

'Well, can you see any sense in chasing after a band of Viking warriors? Even if we find them and manage to engage them, we'll likely lose at least a dozen men just to save the lives of the few poor wretches who've already been taken. What the hell is the point of that?'

'Unfortunately, I don't have any choice,' I told him. 'My father is one of those we're hoping to rescue. Without him to work our small farmstead my mother, my sister and myself will surely starve. Either that or we'll be forced to beg for a living.'

'Even so, you should leave it to us,' he informed me. 'There's no need for you to come unless, of course, you're hell bent on taking revenge yourself.'

'No, I'm not keen on going but don't have any choice. Lord AEthelred himself insisted that I join you. Perhaps I should have helped my father fight off the raiders in the first place. I'm ashamed to say that I merely watched from where I was hiding. They destroyed all they could find then burned our home to the ground. They even killed my dog.'

'Would it have made any difference if you had fought beside your father?'

'Probably not,' I shrugged. 'I could never hope to match his skill as a warrior. But it doesn't seem right to have done nothing to prevent him from being taken.'

He seemed to understand that. 'Aye, well I gather your father is Oswald, who once served in the guard here. It must be difficult to follow a father who has such a formidable reputation.'

'Yes, I sometimes think I must be a great disappointment to him. Did you also know him?'

'No, it was before my time here. But I gather some of the others hold him in very high regard. Do I take it then that this will be your first battle?'

I nodded to confirm that.

'Well, then let's hope that your first is not also your last. But don't worry, Wulfric has reason enough to keep you out of harm's way. If I was you, I'd stay close to him and thereby avoid the worst of the fighting. Senior men like him are never involved in the thickest parts of the fray - unless, of course, we're completely overrun, for then we're all at risk.'

'Surely I must do my share of the fighting?' I insisted.

'If you do, then you're a fool. For my part, I shall be keeping well clear of it if I can. My job will be to track the raiders and hopefully find them before they set sail for their homelands. Beyond that, I'll leave the fighting to those who know the way of it.'

'I hear you're a very good tracker,' I noted.

'Aye, some would say as much. Although I suspect there will be those among the members of the fyrd who will hope that I'm not near as good as my reputation would have it.'

'Why is that?' I asked.

'Because they'd prefer not to find the raiders as that way they won't have to confront them.'

A FOOL'S ERRAND

Having been roused so early by my father the previous morning and then spent much of the day travelling, I slept deeply that night and woke later than I intended. In fact, so much so that I almost missed breakfast and barely had time to grab a cake of bread smeared with honey before rushing out to join the others who were already assembled in the Vill courtyard.

'Good of you to join us,' teased Wulfric, although not unkindly. 'Had you slept any longer you'd have missed us altogether. Or were you planning to follow us in your dreams?'

The men laughed but I took his jibe in good part. With that, I hurriedly looked around at the assembled men but was disappointed by what I saw. My father had often spoken of what it was like to march out as part of a Saxon army with banners flying and the men all eager for battle. What I saw was a group of men who had been pressed into battle as part of the fyrd and had no wish to be there. I was also surprised to find that only Wulfric, Rufus and four of the senior guards would be mounted. Their horses were already saddled but were small, rugged beasts which could be ridden hard across all manner of terrain. Rufus later explained to me that these horses were not trained to the noise and confusion of battle thus, before engaging the enemy, they would be taken to the rear.

As to the rest of the party, the remaining guards were all wearing mail or a protective leather jerkin of one form or another and were equipped with a spear, a shield and a seaxe, whereas the members of the fyrd had donned whatever war gear they had. Their weapons were items they normally used for hunting – spears and bows and such like, plus some which they'd either found discarded on a former battlefield or had perhaps fashioned for themselves.

'Right, form up,' ordered Wulfric. 'We've no more time to waste here and now that Oscar has honoured us with his presence, we should be gone.'

With that, the men lined up in pairs with Wulfric, Rufus and the four mounted guards to the front, followed by the members of the fyrd on foot. The remainder of the guards marched behind them and I was to follow at the back in a small cart which had already been laden with the supplies we would need for the journey, plus some spare war gear and weapons and a goodly supply of arrows.

As we waited for the order to march out, Bishop Leonfric came to bless our endeavours and gave the lead man a banner to carry. It depicted a golden cross which I assumed was intended to imply that what we were doing was God's work. That done, the small party set off.

For our own safety and protection, we were obliged to keep in strict formation but, given that we were travelling across such rough terrain, I struggled to keep up with the others and quickly fell behind.

As Wulfric had warned me, the others were ill inclined to wait for stragglers and although I did my best, the horse pulling the cart seemed to have a mind of its own. In fact, I fell so far behind the column that I struggled to keep close enough to even see it. Eventually, Rufus rode back to help me.

'You're letting that horse have its head,' he warned. 'You need to be firm with it. Accept no nonsense and, if it refuses to do as you command, use the whip to strike it hard across its rump.'

'I'm used to more docile animals,' I explained. 'Our old farm horse had usually been worked so hard that he was too tired to do anything except to wend his own way home.'

'That's all very well, but just remember that this is hostile terrain. And it's not just raiders you need to worry about; that cart load of supplies would make a very tempting target for thieves and robbers so, if I was you, I wouldn't fall too far behind the column. Therefore do as I say. Strike it hard to show it who's master.'

I did as he suggested and pretty soon had the way of it. Rufus then rode alongside me as we tried to catch up with the others. As we did so, I noticed that he, like me, had no war gear or weapons, although he carried a bow slung across his back and had a quiver of arrows attached to his belt. He explained that he'd carefully crafted the arrows himself. They were each fitted with a feather flight and had a head which had been designed for a specific quarry, most of them carved from bone which, being cheap and plentiful, meant he could afford to lose them should he miss his mark. Those with metal heads were more costly and were used only where he could be sure of recovering them to use again.

'A good hunter will always have the right arrow to hand,' he explained. 'For example, for game I would use one of these,' he said, showing me one which had a small rounded head, heavy enough to knock a bird from the air. 'For deer or boar I use the ones which are barbed and keenly sharpened so as to pierce deep into the flesh and remain there even if my quarry then goes to ground. All I have to do is to then follow it until it dies or I can get close enough to despatch it with a spear.'

I noticed one arrow which was quite different to all the others, having a thin metal head, not unlike a nail.'

'Ah!' he said. 'Now that's for very special quarry! As you can see, it's thin enough to penetrate the links in a mail vest so I always carry one just in case I come across a lone Viking raider.'

With that we rejoined the group and continued to follow a track which led towards the coast. We stopped only twice after that to rest and to water the horses, at which time we also ate some of the light provisions of bread and cheese which we'd brought with us. However, Wulfric wouldn't allow us to rest for long as he was anxious to get to the Minster before the raiders and thereby do what he could to protect it.

As we started off again, Wulfric himself rode back along the line to see how I was faring. I was surprised he would do that given that I was probably the least important person in the column.

'Sir, I hope I'm not delaying you?' I offered.

'You're doing well enough,' he assured me. 'But remember what Lord AEthelred said, if this comes to a fray when we get there, stay close to me and do exactly as I say.'

As he spoke, I instinctively fingered the knife which was still tucked inside my belt.

'And don't even think about using that,' he added sternly. 'Like I told you, that won't be near enough whatever your father taught you. If that and your sling are the only weapons you have and you're obliged to confront a Viking warrior, you might just as well kneel down and invite him to strike your head from your shoulders. At least that way you'll get a quicker and more merciful death.'

I hoped he was teasing me but quickly changed the subject. 'Did you then know my father well?' I asked.

'Well enough,' he said. 'And I owe him a great deal, for he once saved my life.'

'Sir, may I ask how that came about?' I ventured.

He seemed reluctant to speak at first. 'Many years ago – when you were still at mother's breast - there was a fray in which we were commanded by Lord AEthelred in person. We'd pursued a band of raiders thinking them to number no more than ten only to find as we confronted them that they were part of a much larger force. Lord AEthelred had sense enough to order us to retreat but, as we did so, my horse stumbled and I fell to the ground, injuring my leg. It's thanks to that that I now walk as I do, for my leg stiffened and now refuses to bend. Anyway, it was your father who rode back to help me. He dismounted and wielded his sword by hacking from left to right and then sweeping it round in an arc so as to keep the Vikings at bay long enough for me to get up. He then climbed back onto his horse and, pulling me up behind him, we made our escape together.'

I remembered seeing my father wielding his sword in just such a manner whilst trying to see off the raiders at our farmstead and mentioned that to Wulfric.

'Aye, well it takes a skilled warrior to fight like that - and a very courageous one given the odds against us that day. He could easily have rode away to save himself as had all the others. Like I say, your father is a very brave man.'

I realised then why Wulfric had helped to persuade Lord AEthelred to rescue my father.

'Anyway,' he continued. 'I would that we had his like with us on this mission. A warband of twenty Vikings we should be able to manage well enough but any more than that and we'll be sorely tested.'

With that, he made his way back along the line, urging the men to hurry as he did so. Soon after that, we could at last see the Minster which was set up high upon a hill in the near distance. Wulfric ordered the column to halt so he could make an initial assessment of our position.

'Sir, is that not smoke I can see?' warned one of the mounted guards.

'Aye,' agreed Wulfric. 'It looks like it. We'll need to get closer to be certain but God forbid that we're too late and find that the Minster has already fallen.'

'Sir, what if the Vikings are still there?' asked one of the men who I think was a member of the fyrd. I couldn't see him from where I was but he sounded nervous.

'Then we'll struggle to prise them out of there without damaging the Minster itself,' replied Wulfric.

'And what if they're not still there, sir?' asked another man.

Wulfric was slow to answer that. 'Then Heaven help us,' he said gravely. 'For if we're to then recover all that's been stolen from the Minster and free the men taken as slaves, we'll have first to find the bastards and then confront them in whatever lair they've found to hole themselves up in. And believe me, that won't be for the faint hearted.'

I LEARN THE HARSH REALITIES OF WAR

What surprised me as we approached the Minster was that it looked to be more like a fortified Vill than a place for Holy servitude. It comprised a cluster of buildings all protected by a tall timber stockade, the gates to which had been broken down and the entrance thereby left wide open. Beyond them we could see the smouldering ruins of several buildings and the stench of smoke hung heavy in the air.

Worried lest the raiders were still inside, Wulfric ordered us all to wait just beyond the stockade but to remain wary. 'It could be a trap,' he warned. 'If they've heard us coming I wouldn't put it past the bastards to conceal themselves ready to take us the moment we pass through what's left of those gates.'

At that, one of the Holy brothers almost tumbled through the entrance to greet us. He kept glancing behind him as though afraid of something then, when he reached Wulfric, he fell to his knees.

'Have the raiders gone?' demanded Wulfric.

'They have, my Lord, but they've left such carnage behind them. It seems that nothing is sacred to such men.'

'Oh, I can believe that right enough! But you're sure that none of them remain?'

'I am, my Lord. All have gone but not before they'd ransacked our Minster and put some of our Holy brethren to the sword.'

'Show me,' ordered Wulfric, but he was in no mind to go rushing in. Still fearing a trap, he ordered us all to remain where we were but had us form up ready to offer him support if needed. Once satisfied with that precaution, he selected two of the mounted guards and had them go with him so that he could assess the position within the stockade for himself.

The two guards positioned themselves on either side of him as they rode through to the inner courtyard, both of them warily watching their flank. After what seemed like an age, one of them retuned to say that it was safe enough for us to proceed, so we all filed in, albeit nervously keeping a careful watch for even the slightest sign of danger.

As soon as we entered the courtyard we could see the full extent of the damage for ourselves. Being built of stone, the monastery itself had withstood the flames well enough but the roof to the Minster was still smouldering as were all the other outbuildings and the stores, including what I took to be a refectory. There were also a dozen or so monks kneeling together in prayer as their lay brothers were busily digging three graves.

'Are you then the abbot here?' demanded Wulfric. He was still mounted as he addressed a man who had remained apart from the others and was fervently praying as he watched those at work.

'I am. And I welcome you to what remains of this Holy place. I am called Father Benedict.'

Wulfric acknowledged that. 'So, father, tell me what happened here.'

Father Benedict shrugged. 'My son, I think you can see that plain enough for yourself,' he answered.

Even as he spoke, I looked at the three bodies which had been laid out on the ground and were being washed ready for burial. They had first been stripped of all their garments so that the wounds they'd suffered were all too plain to see. The first of them had been taken by an axe across his shoulder which had all but severed his arm whereas another had been taken down with an arrow to his chest and another to his side. The third man had been brutally stabbed with a spear, probably whilst cowering on the ground, no doubt pleading for mercy at the time - or perhaps he died on his knees whilst at prayer.

'So, how many raiders were there?' asked Wulfric.

The abbot was slow to answer. 'I would reckon there to have

been at least thirty all told, plus they had with them a dozen poor wretches who had been taken for slaves.'

It was more than we expected but Wulfric made no mention of that for fear of unnerving the men. 'Then it's a wonder that not more of you were taken or slain,' he said, as if to question what Father Benedict had told us.

'We had word of their coming,' explained the good father. 'Thus we took shelter in a small grove of trees beyond the hill. These three good brothers insisted on remaining here to protect our Minster which is dedicated to the service and memory of St Matthew.'

Wulfric seemed unimpressed with that. 'A curious choice of benefactor. Was he not the disciple who was once a tax collector before becoming one of our Lord's disciples?'

Father Benedict smiled. 'That's true, but is it not proof enough that we can all of us repent our past sufficient to then serve the Lord? Hence that's the premise on which our order was founded. Many of us here take much solace from that as we each of us repent our worldly sins.'

'Much good that patronage did these poor souls,' mused Wulfric looking at the bodies.

'They died for something which is more precious to us than life itself,' explained the abbot.

'Did they? And what would that be?'

'Why, the Holy relics and the items which are such an important part of our worship here,' said the abbot, sounding surprised. 'Amongst other things, the raiders took a reliquary which contained no less than a finger of St Matthew himself, not to mention a solid gold cross and several silver platters engraved with the Holy image of Christ.'

'Well, probably better dead than being taken. But surely their sacrifice was in vain?'

'It was God's will that they should perish thus and at least they'll be well received in the life to come. But pray tell me, what brings you to this place?' he asked. 'Your arrival is welcome, albeit belated.'

'We've come in pursuit of the raiders who attacked you but are obviously too late. I must therefore ask whether or not they knew we were coming?'

'I doubt it, my son. After all, it's well known that these heathens relish the chance for slaughter so would surely have stayed if they did. By my reckoning they left here but an hour ago heading due south towards the coast. I assume they have a longship there but, by the time they reach it, it'll be too late for them to board and set sail tonight. Most likely they'll depart these shores tomorrow on the morning tide.'

'Thank you,' said Wulfric. 'Then we could yet be in time to reach them.'

'Is that wise, my son? Surely, you're not thinking to engage them?'

'Those are my orders. Hence, with your permission, we'll rest here for a while whilst we decide what next to do.'

'Gladly,' said the abbot. 'Then will you and your men not share our meagre supper whilst you wait?'

'Thank you, father. If you've food enough for us all, then we'd welcome whatever fare your table has to offer - though even that may be scant comfort to us given what fate we may well be obliged to confront tomorrow.'

THE LOGISTICS OF BATTLE

Several of our men helped to finish digging graves for the poor souls who had been slain whilst others set about dealing with the aftermath of the fires by pulling down those buildings which were beyond salvage and then clearing away the debris. That done, we quickly established a sort of makeshift camp in the courtyard where we would be protected by the stockade, albeit the gates had not been repaired so that the entrance remained wide open. Hence guards were posted to keep watch through the night whilst Rufus lit a substantial fire around which we all huddled as proof against the cold. As we sat there, the monks brought us bowls of steaming broth together with large crusts of stale bread which was washed down with ale they'd brewed for themselves and which they'd somehow managed to hide from the raiders.

'Are you not supposed to be the best hunter in all of Wessex?' asked one of the men looking at Rufus.

'I am,' replied Rufus.

'Then why in God's name haven't you caught us something more substantial to fill our bellies?'

Rufus just grinned. 'What would you have? A deer or perhaps some game?' he asked good naturedly.

'A wild boar would be better!' roared the man, which others all agreed would be their choice as well.

'Ah! I'll not go chasing after wild boar in the dark, for they're a dangerous quarry and not easy to take unless you know the way of it. I recall that on one occasion I came across some boar in a forest. They were coming towards me in a line so I quickly climbed a tree to avoid them and, as they passed beneath me, I couldn't resist taking a shot with my bow, aiming at the one which was leading the others. It proved to be a grave mistake.'

'Why so?' asked the man.

'I've since learned that the lead animal is usually the boar whilst the others are his sows who will follow him anywhere. You can kill as many sows as you will but if you kill the boar they'll turn on you for certain and never let you alone until they've had their revenge. I would have been forced to remain in that tree all night had the rest of the hunting party not come looking for me. Even then, it was the devil's own job to drive them off and, in the end, we had to kill them all. Since then, I'm always wary of hunting for wild pigs.'

At first no one seemed sure whether or not to take what he'd said seriously, that is until Wulfric spoke up. 'What Rufus says is true. My father was a woodsman and he warned me about shooting boar. They can be among the most dangerous animals in the forest. Perhaps second only to wolves.'

'Or bears,' said Rufus. 'You wouldn't want to confront a bear.'

'When did you last see a bear in these parts?' chided Wulfric, laughing.

Rufus had to admit that bears had become very scarce, although he added that he'd heard tell of some in the mountains and forests beyond the great dyke.

With that, all the men took it in turns to tell stories, most of which were taken from a rich store of such tales which formed part of our Saxon heritage. As was our way, we then debated the meaning or the moral of each story, even though this was often open to interpretation – and usually a good deal of argument as well!

I had no story to tell and, in any event, felt too timid to join in the conversation. I therefore took to counting the members of our band and found that it comprised thirty-eight men all told, including myself, which meant that we were still a match for the raiders. I mentioned that to Wulfric.

'Aye,' he said. 'We're pretty much even in terms of numbers, but not in terms of experience. Apart from the Vill guards, these men are farmers or tradesmen pressed into service,' he reminded me. 'They're brave enough and have some weapon skills between them but are no match for a Viking warband. Hence I'm concerned about proceeding further.'

'But the raiders will likely be gone if we delay!' I complained.

That was certainly true. The abbot had estimated that the coast was at most two hour's march from there and, whilst we still had no idea where they'd hidden their longship, it was unlikely to be far away. That meant that they could well set sail without even knowing we were in pursuit of them.

'So what would you have me do?' demanded Wulfric. 'Attack them in the dark? If we do that we'll risk losing even more men than we're likely to save!'

I was disappointed given the debt he owed my father and so spoke without thinking. 'Then I'll go on alone,' I announced boldly, regretting the words almost as soon as they were spoken.

Those who heard me laughed. 'Boy, they'll kill you before you can draw that knife from your belt!' warned one of the men.

'Aye,' said another. 'Or more likely they'll take you to join your father as a slave. Why the hell would you risk them doing that?'

'At least I'll have done what I can to free my father,' I reasoned.

Again they all laughed. 'Then you're a fool! Have you any inkling of a what a Viking warband can do? They're bloodthirsty pagans who thrive on cruelty and torture. What's more, they can be very inventive when it comes to inflicting pain!'

'I know full well what they're like!' I retorted sharply. 'It's been scarce two days since I watched as they took my father away. He was a proud man and, as some of you well know, not a warrior who would give up without a fight. Yet he and our farmhand were overwhelmed, beaten almost senseless and then dragged away to be sold as slaves. What's more, our farmstead was ransacked, looted and then burned to the ground. Do you expect me to do nothing to avenge all that? Would you have me sit here with you beside this fire, idly telling each other tales? Besides, what sort of men would we be to leave these raiders free to destroy other Saxon homes, killing and pillaging at will when we have the chance to set matters to rights?'

The last point struck home and everyone was silent for a moment, as if letting my words sink in.

'There's precious little we can do except perhaps to drive them off,' said Wulfric. 'And what would be the point of that given they'll likely leave of their own accord in the morning if left alone? Either way, that will be of no comfort to your father, nor will it enable us to recover whatever they've looted from this Holy place or from Saxon homes, but it is the way of it. We must always weigh up the odds against us and thereby assess the risk. That's the logistics of battle.'

'For you perhaps,' I challenged. 'But I'm not so easily daunted. At the very least I'll creep into their camp whilst it's still dark and try to free my father.'

'You'll be butchered if they catch you,' he replied.

'What of it? At least I'll die like a true Saxon, which is what I'm sure my father would do – and what you should do as well!' I'm not sure where my courage came from except that I was angry at having come so far for nothing. Rufus had described it as a "fool's errand" but it now seemed that the only fool there was me!

Wulfric looked at me as if not sure what he could say to sway me. 'You have your father's courage, I'll give you that. But Oscar, I fear you'll be throwing your life away for nothing. Surely that's not what he would want?'

'It's true that my father would have his views on that just as I have mine,' I said firmly. 'But I'm not concerned about what he'll think of me; it's what I'll think of myself if I do nothing which worries me.' With that I looked to Rufus who I had come to like. 'Will you at least help me to find the raider's camp?' I asked.

He considered that for a moment. 'I will,' he answered, choosing his words with care. 'But I agree with what's been said. Only a fool would take them on single handed so I'll not join you in that part of your plan. Nor will I wait around to watch you die.'

I then turned to Wulfric again. 'Given all you told me about what my father once did for you, can I not persuade you to come with me as far as the coast and at least see how things are set before giving up so easily?'

For a moment Wulfric didn't answer. 'Very well,' he decided. 'Gather up your things all of you. We've all eaten and rested so we'll leave at once.'

None of the others seemed keen on the idea of marching out in the dark. 'We should wait till morning,' grumbled one of the men, speaking for them all.

'You have my orders,' insisted Wulfric. 'We have a job to do and, having come thus far, we can't now let this boy go on alone to do it for us.'

'Why the hell not? It's his father we've come to rescue,' pressed the man.

'Because we've been ordered to intercept these raiders by no less than Ealdorman AEthelred himself, that's why. If nothing else, we should at least try to recover all they've stolen from here and from other Saxon homes, not to mention avenge the good members of this Holy order we've just helped to bury.'

OUR PLAN FOR THE IMPENDING BATTLE

Based on what the abbot had told us, we were certain that we could reach the coast within a few hours and thus be there well before dawn. Therefore, whilst reluctant to leave the warmth of the fire, we all wrapped ourselves up in our cloaks as best we could and prepared to march out at once. Knowing that the terrain between there and the coast was likely to be rough, we left the cart at the Minster and all travelled on foot so as not to get separated in the dark. Even Wulfric and the guards dismounted but they took their horses with them in case they were needed. As we went, some of the men lit torches which were shared between us yet, even in such poor light, Rufus managed to find enough of a trail left by the raiders for us to follow.

'How does he do it?' I asked Wulfric.

'Lord only knows,' he replied. 'It's the same when he goes hunting. He sees the signs which most of us would miss and sometimes follows them for hours to find his quarry. It's a God given skill which few men possess, that's for sure.'

'So is he a good hunter?'

'No, he's much more than that,' said Wulfric. 'He's probably the best hunter in all Wessex! Not only has he learned the skill of how to track and follow a trail over almost any terrain, he also has what seems to be a second sight which enables him to find his way around a forest even when it's one where he's never hunted before.'

After an hour or so the terrain began to change and we eventually found ourselves on a sandy track with dunes heaped up around us, some of them near shoulder height. Pretty soon we could all of us hear the sound of the sea in the distance.

'Their trail leads down onto the beach,' Rufus told us. 'They can't be far from here as I can smell the smoke from their campfire. We'd best not disturb them too soon so everyone wait here whilst I try to find them. And for God's sake keep those horses quiet!'

With that he went off into the darkness on his own, moving so quietly that he was almost like a shadow. He returned a short time later. 'It's as I thought,' he announced, his voice not much more than a whisper. 'Their camp is just over there, tucked away in one of the hollows where they think they won't be seen. There are about thirty of them, but they all appear to be sleeping close to their fire with just two men on guard. The prisoners are all roped together at the edge of the camp.'

'So, what will we do?' asked one of the men sounding worried.

'We'll wait,' said Wulfric firmly. 'We can't risk fighting in the dark. We also need to know where they've hidden their longship. Rufus, go down to the beach to see if you can find any sign of that as well. It won't be far from here, though will likely be well hidden.'

With that, Rufus slipped away into the night once more but then returned more quickly than we expected. 'Their ship is moored not far along the beach,' he assured us. 'It's plain enough having been dragged up from the shoreline and is now secured to a stake driven into the sand. I assume they fetched it from wherever they'd hidden it and have already loaded it ready to set sail as soon as the tide allows.'

'So you think all their loot's now on board?' asked Wulfric.

'Aye, most likely it is. If so, it's guarded by just two men who we could take easily enough. If once we've recovered what's on board we then cut the mooring rope, the ship will drift out to sea when the tide turns. That way all the raiders will be stranded and…'

'No,' insisted Wulfric, not letting him finish. 'Whatever options we have we must wait for it to get light enough for us to see what the hell we're doing. These are warriors who have been tried and tested in battle more times than we can count so I won't take any chances. Besides, the last thing we want is to leave a band of raiders stranded here. God knows what the murderous bastards would get up to!'

* * *

As we waited for the dawn, Wulfric questioned Rufus about the ship.

'Well, it's definitely a longship,' confirmed Rufus. 'Not just some trading vessel. I've not seen one up close before but it looks to be big enough for them all and as many prisoners as they're inclined to carry with them.'

'Yes, that's what worries me,' said Wulfric. 'We've had no reports of them looting for the supplies they'd need to sail back to their homelands, so does that mean they've not yet done with raids here in Wessex? If that is the case, I fear that once they leave here they may strike again elsewhere along the coast. You say their ship has been dragged up onto the beach? If so, they'll need to wait on the tide before they can relaunch it which would be a very good time for us to attack.'

'I don't know about that,' said Rufus who didn't seem convinced. 'I've heard it said that these ships can navigate in very shallow water. All they'll need to do is drag it a little way out to sea then float it off. A competent crew should be able to manage that well enough, particularly with slaves to help them.'

'Then we'll attack at first light when they least expect it,' announced Wulfric. 'They don't yet know we're here so we'll have the element of surprise. We'll go down to the beach and form a shield wall in front of the ship. Once we're set, the mounted guards supported by a few others will then ride into their camp and drive them out. They'll think there are more of us than there are and so will retreat to their ship where the rest of us will be waiting, armed and ready.'

'The horses will struggle in the soft sand which will surely slow us down,' complained one of the Vill guards who would be one of those forming the mounted assault. 'Besides, not being used to the noise of a battle, the horses could become unsettled. If the Vikings see that they'll likely turn on us and put us all to the sword. What's more, the rest of you will fare no better. Once they've done with us, you'll be left waiting on the beach for your turn to be slaughtered!'

Even Wulfric admitted that was a risk, particularly as it would mean splitting our force.

'There might be a better way,' I found myself saying.

Suddenly all eyes were on me. 'And what might that be?' asked Wulfric, almost laughing.

It was a strange thing as I'd not actually thought about what I was about to say, yet somehow I seemed to know what we had to do and could see the battle plan as clearly as if it were laid out before me. I can't explain it any more than that, except that it probably stemmed from all the stories my father had told me about the battles in which he'd fought, thereby giving me some insight in such matters - even though I'd never seen a battle before, never mind actually fought in one! 'What if I creep down to the camp and release the bonds of all the slaves,' I suggested. 'Whilst I'm about it, I could leave a few spears and bows just beyond the camp where they can reach them.'

'How the hell will that help us?' asked one of the men.

'At dawn, we'll go down and form the shield wall in front of their ship, just as Wulfric has suggested,' I continued. 'Once awake, the raiders will see us on the beach and have no option but to attack us if they want to reach their ship. Besides, they'll regard us as an easy target and as a chance to take more slaves – or to quench whatever thirst for blood they still have.'

'But we'd be sitting ducks!' said Wulfric.

'Not if as they attack you, the prisoners take up the weapons I've left for them and assault the raiders from behind. They won't be expecting that and, with warriors like my father among the prisoners, they won't stand a chance.'

Wulfric looked stunned at what I was suggesting. 'How the hell did you come up with that idea?' he stormed.

'Would my plan not work?' I asked somewhat sheepishly, fearing I'd made a fool of myself.

Suddenly his face broke into a broad grin. 'Oh, I think it could work right enough. In fact, I think it could work very well indeed,' he said. 'They'll have to take us on if they want to reach their ship so, if we limit the shield wall to just the Vill guards, that will make a very tempting target. The rest of you can lie low in the dunes on either side of what will become the battlefield and keep yourselves from being seen. When they attack us, you can spring out and loose arrows into their midst then attack from both flanks at once. With that, the shield wall to the front of them and having to contend with the armed prisoners attacking from the rear, they'll be caught like rats in a trap!'

At first no one spoke.

'This is our chance to give them a taste of Saxon vengeance,' stressed Wulfric anxious to secure everyone's support.

Still not all the others seemed to agree. 'More likely we'll get ourselves killed,' warned one man. 'We should just let Oscar creep down into the camp to free his father then be gone from here.'

'Aye, if not we'll all end up as slaves ourselves,' complained another. 'Either that or we'll all be killed.'

Wulfric could see that he needed to ensure their support. 'Yes,' he said. 'But don't forget, if Oscar's plan works, we should be able to seize their ship intact and also recover all the booty they've stowed on board. That alone will mean a goodly share for each of us if we succeed.'

The prospect of earning a share of any booty was always at the forefront of everyone's mind when fighting as part of the fyrd, so mention of the ship as a prize was enough to sway even the doubtful souls as its value alone would be very significant indeed.

With no one expressing any further concerns, Wulfric set about deciding who would stand where. 'Those with bows should take up a position on the flanks either side of the battlefield, but stay hidden until I give the word,' he ordered, refining his plan even as he spoke. 'The rest of you can form the shield wall with the members of the fyrd standing behind the Vill guards.' He then turned to me. 'Oscar, if you're going down to free the prisoners you run the gravest risk. Are you prepared for that?'

It was a worrying thought and not something I'd fully considered when I first suggested it. Nonetheless, I was by then resolved to see it through. 'If I'm taken, I'll tell them that I came looking for my father, nothing more. They'll therefore be none the wiser about our plans. Presumably you'll be able to free me in the morning with all the other slaves once the raiders have been defeated?' I added, somewhat hopefully.

'Yes, provided they don't kill you first,' warned Wulfric.

'Why would they do that? Surely, I'm worth more to them as a slave?'

'Perhaps. But you can never be sure of anything when it comes to the Vikings. They'll just as likely think they have enough slaves already and kill you just for the pleasure of watching you squirm in agony as you die.'

I RISK TRYING TO FREE MY FATHER

By my reckoning, there was at least an hour before it got light which meant there was still time enough for me to risk going down into the Vikings' camp. Thus, with Wulfric's permission, Rufus and I crept through the dunes whilst keeping ourselves hidden as best we could. We took with us half a dozen spears and several bows, together with quivers containing as many arrows as could be spared. The plan was for Rufus to show me the way then cover me with his bow in case I was spotted. Whilst it was a comfort to know he was there, my concern was that if he was forced to shoot, the raiders would then know that I was not alone. That would put Wulfric and the others at risk of being seen and our plan would thereby be thwarted - and with it, any hope of me being rescued in the morning!

'Can you protect me from here?' I asked Rufus as we breasted one of the dunes from where we could look down onto the part of the camp where the prisoners were being held.

'Yes, given a clear shot I can take down one or two of them if I have to,' he assured me. 'But for God's sake be as quick and as careful as you can, for once they're woken there'll be hell to pay!'

With that, I crept carefully forwards then slid down across the face of the dune on my back until I was crouched at the very edge of the Vikings' camp. By then, there was just enough light for me to see, albeit not as clearly as I would have liked. Even so, it was all just as Rufus had reported; all the raiders appeared to be sleeping soundly, including two men who I assumed were supposed to be keeping watch. A little way away from me were the prisoners themselves, all roped together and looking very forlorn. Most important of all, I could see my father among them and knew that I would get just one chance to free him. Although it seemed a fearful risk, it was one I had no option but to take so I therefore began to edge as close to him as I dared, then crawled the last few vital yards on my hands and knees, desperately trying not to disturb anyone.

'Father,' I whispered when I reached him. 'It's me, Oscar. I've come for you.'

As he stirred, I was afraid he might be startled and thereby betray my presence so I gently covered his mouth with my hand. 'I'm here to free you all,' I said softly.

With that he was awake but the look in his eyes was one of sheer astonishment.

'You young fool! Get away from here whilst you can!' he hissed.

I didn't answer but instead drew my knife and cut through his bonds. 'Stay as you are and pretend you're sleeping,' I insisted. 'Wulfric is here with others and we have a plan. When the raiders see him and the fyrd on the beach, they'll have no option but to attack if they mean to reach their ship. As they do so, you need to hit them from behind.'

'What, single handed and unarmed?' he hissed, sounding incredulous.

'No, I mean to free you all and I've left some weapons just beyond the dunes over there for you to use. But don't make a move until the raiders attack us. Our plan is to take them by surprise and hit them hard from all sides at once.'

'This is madness,' warned my father. 'What the hell are you doing here? Did I not charge you with looking out for your mother and Odelia!'

'They're fine. And did you really think I'd leave you to be taken for a slave?'

When he didn't answer that I moved onto the next prisoner and then the next. I'd almost freed them all when one of the prisoners was so pleased at the chance to get away that he got up and tried to make a run for it on his own. Of course, he was seen by one of the raiders almost at once and taken down by an arrow to his back. Even as he fell, I heard someone yell out and knew then that I'd been spotted as well.

I wasn't sure what to do. It was getting light by then and my instinct was to run for the cover of the dunes but I knew that if I did, I'd likely get an arrow in my back as well. I therefore got up and raised my hands, hoping that Rufus would go to tell Wulfric what had happened. If he did, then all I had to do was to survive until dawn.

* * *

With my hands raised, I moved away from the other prisoners, anxious to ensure that the raiders wouldn't notice that their bonds had been cut. Before doing so, I discreetly dropped my knife close to where my father lay so that he might use it to free the few prisoners I hadn't managed to reach.

Needless to say, I was treated none too well. Those among the raiders who were awake by then began jeering and taunting me as one of them struck me hard across the face, knocking me to the ground. He then kicked me repeatedly in the ribs and belly. I was saved from an even worse beating when one of the raiders appeared at the far end of the camp and began shouting. Of course, I couldn't understand what he was saying but suddenly the others were all wide awake and shaking off their blankets. Once on their feet, they hurriedly grabbed their weapons and shields and began rushing towards the beach, not even bothering with the rest of their war gear as they sensed the prospect of booty, blood or yet more slaves. More importantly, to a man they seemed to be enthralled by the heady scent of battle.

As this was happening, I lay on the ground, half expecting to be killed at any moment. I couldn't understand what had alerted the raiders and my only hope was that Rufus had managed to reach Wulfric and the others in time, thereby enabling them to hurriedly prepare their defence. However, that was the least of my worries. Of more concern to me was that the man who had beaten me seemed torn between killing me or joining the others in the blood fest on the beach. I stared up at him and could see from the look in his eyes that either way he intended to finish me. Then, as he raised an axe ready to strike, all I could do was utter a short prayer and wait for the blow which I knew would surely follow.

THE BATTLE UNFOLDS

My mother used to assure me that if I was earnest in saying my prayers they would surely be answered - although I suspect that what happened next had little to do with that. All I recall was staring up at the man who was about to kill me with an axe. Then, for no obvious reason, I saw the look on his face change from that of blood lust to one of pain and sheer surprise. He turned away from me, staggered a few uncertain steps then fell to lie face down in the sand. When I looked again I could see my father standing over him, the knife I'd given him held tight in his hand and the blade smeared with blood.

My father reached down and helped me to my feet. 'Oscar, are you harmed?' he asked earnestly.

'No father. At least, not seriously,' I assured him, ignoring the fact that my ribs felt very sore and bruised from the beating I'd taken. At that I looked around and saw that the camp was all but deserted save for the prisoners, all of whom were on their feet. I explained to my father where I'd left the weapons I'd brought with me and he sent three men to retrieve them and then hand them round. Even as that was being done, we heard the unmistakeable sounds of shouting coming from beyond the dunes.

'What's Wulfric's plan?' asked my father hurriedly.

'He wants you to wait until the raiders assault his shield wall then attack them from behind. That way you'll trap them between you. But we'll need to be closer than this or they'll have time to see us coming,' I told him.

My father seemed pleased at the prospect. 'Good,' he said, turning to share that news with the others. 'We all of us have a score to settle with these heathen bastards.' He then led us towards the beach so that we could watch from behind one of the dunes as the battle began to unfold.

* * *

As we watched, I realised that on seeing me taken, Rufus must have indeed returned and reported that to Wulfric who had immediately formed his battle lines but, in so doing, they'd been spotted. When I looked across to where the raiders' ship was still moored, I could see the bodies of the two men who had been set to guard it, both stretched out on the sand beside the hull, each with an arrow in his chest. I smiled when I realised that was almost certainly the handiwork of Rufus.

Meanwhile, Wulfric had ordered his men to form their lines ready for battle. The shield wall was our usual response to any attack as it offered protection and also served to at least slow down and possibly halt any assault. He'd placed the members of the Vill guard in the front row with their shields interlocked as they'd been trained to do, with the members of the fyrd standing directly behind them. The bowmen had not had time to take up their position on either flank but that didn't seem to matter, they were equally well placed, forming a third row at the back. The plan was simple and well-rehearsed – the front row would block the assault whilst those standing behind them would thrust their spears through the gaps in the wall of shields, trying to kill or wound the attackers. It could be devastatingly effective but it depended on the whole unit fighting and moving as one. Any breach would mean that the wall could be opened up which would result in carnage.

The raiders would have no doubt encountered a Saxon shield wall before, certainly often enough to know how best to deal with it. Normally they would have formed themselves into a "wedge" so that they could hit the wall hard at whatever point they judged to be weakest, then fan out along its entire length, hacking and thrusting with their weapons as they did so. However, from what I could see, they hadn't troubled to prepare their assault. They must have seen at once that what they were up against was nothing more than a dozen trained men and a rabble of others who barely knew what they were about. Yet that small band had managed to block access to their ship and therefore had to be dealt with if they were to stand any chance of using it to sail away with their slaves and booty intact. What they didn't know at that stage was that those slaves were all free by then and not only armed, but also craving vengeance.

My father urged us all to wait. 'Let them fully engage before we strike,' he ordered having taken charge of the band. 'When we do, we move quietly towards them with no shouting or battle cries as we don't want them to hear us coming until it's too late. That way we'll retain the element of surprise.'

From there, we all watched as the raiders began to advance on Wulfric's small band, still jeering and shouting their own challenges as they closed upon them. Then, from within the Saxon ranks, someone began to shout the Saxon war cry of OUT! OUT! OUT! Others quickly took up the chant, all of them shouting it as loud as they could until it seemed to resound across the beach in the cold, early morning air.

It was then that the battle began in earnest.

* * *

We could only watch as the raiders surged forward, screaming and shouting their abuse but, even as they did so, the bowmen behind the shield wall took their cue from Rufus and loosed their arrows into the air. Given they numbered so few, what followed could hardly be described as a barrage but, even so, it accounted for at least three Vikings. More importantly, it slowed the advance of the others as they were forced to take shelter beneath their shields. Wulfric left the bowmen to shoot at will whilst he then focused on the shield wall itself, urging our men to remain steadfast and to ready themselves for the onslaught which they all knew would follow.

'Wait!' ordered my father, still anxious lest we made our move too soon.

What followed was like nothing I'd ever seen. The raiders slammed home their attack, hitting the wall of Saxon shields so hard that the men who faced them seemed to stagger back under the weight of the assault. Then, as the raiders began to spread out, they started hacking at our men with their swords and axes. They were held back at that stage as the Saxons probed them with spears but, every so often, one of them managed to force a gap in our ranks and break through, but always at the cost of his own life. I watched as some men turned away from the fray to tend their wounds, whilst others simply fell and died. What I couldn't see at that stage was how our men were faring. I could only assume that some of them had died or been wounded as well.

It was then that my father ordered us to attack.

'Right, we go now!' he said quietly and, with that, led the way down the beach. Even though unarmed, I followed them, albeit I held back, still nursing my ribs following the beating I'd already taken. Then, as we slammed into the rear of them, we wrought more carnage than I believed possible. Fearing to turn and engage us lest they were killed by the men standing behind the shield wall, the raiders were all but defenceless and were quickly despatched. Some of them broke off and tried to make a run for it along the beach but Rufus quickly put paid to that and had his men take them down with arrows before they could get far enough away.

Having been ordered to avoid the fray, I still held back only to be confronted by a man who had been wounded by an arrow to his side. He had no axe nor even a shield but nonetheless still seemed intent on fighting. As he drew a seaxe from his belt, he no doubt saw in me an easy target. Being unarmed, I wasn't sure what best to do as I had no way of defending myself - but then remembered my sling. He all but laughed when I produced it although that changed when I hurriedly loosed a stone which struck his forehead. He swayed for a moment, hardly able to believe what had happened, then fell to the ground.

'Finish him!' said a voice from somewhere behind me. I recognised it as that of old Seth, our farmhand.

'Finish him and be done with it!' By then Seth was standing right beside me, proffering a knife which he had no doubt taken from one of the men he'd killed. 'If you leave him you'll only have to fight him again. Or someone else will.'

I understood what he was saying but still couldn't do it. In the end, Seth was obliged to kill the man for me, stepping forward and slitting his throat with the knife.

THE AFTERMATH OF BATTLE

The battle carried on until Wulfric at last ordered us to stop. When we did, it was clear that most of the raiders were either dead or so badly wounded that they could no longer fight on.

'Put the survivors to the sword,' said Wulfric coldly. 'We've no provision for taking prisoners.'

The men were only too eager to oblige. What followed was nothing short of wanton slaughter and I could barely bring myself to watch as they brutally despatched the survivors with whatever weapon came to hand.

Whilst that was going on, Wulfric greeted my father warmly.

'A timely arrival,' said my father as they clasped hands.

'Aye, thanks to your son. It was him who persuaded us to come in the first place.'

My father looked surprised. 'Did he by God,' was all he said.

Wulfric grinned. 'Yes, and what's more, he has an eye for the tactics of a battle as our plan was mostly his idea as well. It seems he follows in his father's steps and thus has the makings of a warrior.'

My father didn't seem to know what to make of that but, before he could say anything, Seth, having overheard them, intervened. 'I grant you that he fights well enough and has the guts for a battle but as yet he's a little squeamish,' he teased, recalling how I'd left him to finish off the man I'd felled with my sling.

* * *

With the fighting over and the battle won, the men began searching the bodies for small items of plunder – particularly rings, silver armbands and anything else of value, all of which they would no doubt tuck away as "personal" plunder if they could do so without Wulfric seeing. If I said very little at this point it was because I felt guilty about the loss of five members of the fyrd who had all been brutally killed, not to mention all those who had been wounded.

'It's the price we pay for battle,' mused Wulfric, sensing my disquiet. 'Whether we win or lose, there are always casualties to be reckoned with.'

I still said nothing but instead went to join my father and Seth.

'So, your mother and sister are both safe?' asked my father as we sat together on the beach.

'They are, father,' I assured him. 'They're staying with Uncle Oswin. It was he who gave me that knife.'

'Then what of our farmstead? I imagine the raiders destroyed it?'

I could hardly bring myself to answer that as I recalled the sight of our home in flames and all our belongings scattered or broken on the ground. 'At least they didn't take the livestock,' I managed. 'But I wish I'd done more to help you and Seth to fight them off.'

'Don't worry son. You did what was needed. Had you joined me your mother would have stayed as well and then we'd all of us been slain or taken,' he said consolingly.

'But it cost so many lives,' I said as I looked across at the bodies of our men which had been laid out so they could be returned to their families.

My father seemed to know exactly what was troubling me. 'Don't worry, after a battle we all of us feel as you do now. We regret what was done in the heat of combat and, in particular, the blood that was shed. But then, when the time comes, we'll all of us fight again readily enough, just as I did today despite all my misgivings. That's one reason why I wanted you to avoid serving in the fyrd – that and the prospect of seeing you needlessly slain.'

'I think I understand that now,' I admitted. 'But it all seems such a pointless waste.'

'Exactly. There are better ways of making a living than by risking your life in some pointless battle for someone else's cause. I often wonder how many of the men I've slain might have become friends had I met them elsewhere rather than on a battlefield. But think on this, what we've achieved today may at least deter other raiders from coming here to pillage and murder honest Saxons, so perhaps those good men over there didn't die for nothing.'

'Is that all we've achieved from spilling so much blood?' I asked.

He thought about that for a moment. 'No, not just that. You'll have also earned a goodly reward for your part in recovering the booty and for taking that ship intact. That may suffice to help us rebuild our farmstead. Mind, whatever reward is due will need to be shared with the others who took part in the battle, including the families of those who died.'

Even that seemed little enough to convince me that what we'd done was worth it.

'There is one other thing,' said my father.

I looked at him, not sure what he was referring to.

'I suspect you've now earned yourself a place in the fyrd whether you like it or not. I never wanted that for you but I fear there will now be no way to avoid it, so you'd best get used to all this killing. God forbid that you should ever come to like it.'

* * *

By then, some of the men had dug a pit in the sand in which to bury the dead Vikings, their bodies being tossed into it having first been stripped of their war gear. Most of that was taken by the members of the fyrd to use when next they were called upon to fight.

Meanwhile, some of the other men prepared to use the horses to carry our wounded back to the Minster where they could be tended by the monks.

'Tell the good abbot that I'll come myself once we've finished here and will then return the items which were stolen from the Minster,' said Wulfric.

As the remainder of us rested, Rufus came across to speak with me. 'Your plan worked well,' he enthused. 'But I have to say, I thought you would be killed when they caught you freeing the prisoners.'

'So did I,' I admitted. 'But I was lucky. My father slew the man who was intent on butchering me with his axe.' At that, I looked to my father but he said nothing.

'Even so, it's one of the rare occasions when we've managed to get the better of a band of raiders. I think Lord AEthelred will be much pleased with you, as are all the men as they'll be well rewarded for their part in the victory.'

* * *

It was later that Wulfric came across to join my father and myself once more. 'I think this belongs to you,' he said to my father as he handed him back his sword. 'I recognised it when it was found beside one of the dead raiders. We've also recovered their haul of booty which, as Rufus rightly guessed, had been stored aboard their ship.'

My father took the sword and examined it almost reverently, clearly pleased to have it back.

'Is that the sword you wielded whilst a member of the permanent guard at the Vill?' I asked.

'Aye it is,' said my father. 'As you know, I served there for many years when I was younger, as did my father before me. But it was no way for a man to live, hence I took to farming instead. God knows that's a hard way to put food on the table but it's better than all this pointless slaughter. Surely any father would want something better for his son than that?'

At that Wulfric put his hand on my shoulder. 'Yet your son did well,' he said. 'But for him both you and Seth would now be slaves. As I said, the plan was also his idea and he even proved himself in the battle. He has more guts than most men, that's for sure. You've reason enough to be proud of him.'

'I am,' said my father. 'Although I wish he hadn't been forced to risk his life to hear me say it.'

* * *

On closer inspection it turned out that Rufus had been right about the Viking ship. It wasn't one of the smaller vessels which the Vikings used for coastal trading and for ferrying supplies and such like. Rather it was a proper longship with a prow which was carved into the shape of a fearsome dragon and with rowing benches for thirty men. Wulfric advised us that a fleet of such vessels had crossed the seas to the north as part of an invasion which had already conquered Mercia, Northumbria and the land of the East Saxons.

'Are you thinking what I'm thinking?' asked Wulfric, clearly concerned as he and Rufus examined the ship.

'That this band was more than just a raiding party?' offered Rufus.

'Exactly. With a ship like this they could well be part of the Viking army which is now in Mercia. Perhaps pickings there are getting slim given how many of them there are there and this band has therefore ventured further afield. If so, it could be the first of many.'

'God preserve us if that's the way of it.'

As we considered the implications of that, one member of the fyrd who was a carpenter by trade had been asked to look over the ship to assess its condition. 'She needs some minor repair,' he reported, 'but she seems sound enough.'

Wulfric then asked if any of us had any experience of sailing but didn't seem surprised to find that there was no one among us who had. 'It's of no matter,' he mused. 'It takes an experienced crew to manage these vessels under sail. They can be rowed but it would take at least twenty men at the oars and we can't spare near enough men for that, particularly if none of us know what we're about. I'll therefore send word to one of the coastal settlements as perhaps they can put this vessel to good use. In the meantime, make up some litters so we can carry our dead back to the Vill and thereby return them to their families for a Christian burial.'

OUR TRIUMPHANT RETURN TO THE VILL

Two of the Vill guards were detailed to remain with the captured longship whilst another was sent to a nearby coastal settlement to see what use could be made of the vessel. In the meantime, Wulfric had kept back one of the horses onto which we loaded all the plunder we'd recovered from the raiders. Whilst there was a lot of it, most of it looked to have been stolen from churches and would therefore need to be returned and the rest didn't amount to much in terms of value as it had been looted from modest farmsteads. As we then marched back to the Minster, it was a somewhat sombre procession as few of us were in the mood for talking; although there were some who seemed intent on retelling of their exploits during the battle to anyone who would listen. For my part, I ignored them all and walked instead with my father and Seth, neither of whom had much to say about what had transpired either.

When we reached the Minster, Father Benedict came forth to greet us in person, no doubt anxious to reclaim what had been stolen from his order. Wulfric first insisted on seeing our wounded, most of whom had been well tended by the monks and had recovered enough to at least stand unaided, although several were still in considerable pain and couldn't be moved.

'Those who are seriously wounded should remain here for now,' insisted the abbot. 'There are members of our order who have the skills needed to tend them, including a knowledge of herbs and such like which should aid their recovery. Once healed sufficient to travel, we'll see them safely back to their homes.'

'Thank you, father,' said Wulfric.

The good abbot brushed aside his thanks saying that it was the least they could do for those who had helped to recover their sacred possessions.

With that, Wulfric took the hint and had one of the men unpack the items which we'd placed on the packhorse and spread them out on the ground.

The abbot readily acknowledged that only part of it had been taken from the Minster. He identified the reliquary containing the finger of St Matthew plus a heavy gold cross and several silver platters, all of which he'd earlier listed as items which had been taken. He also picked up some beautiful coloured pages which had been torn from several Holy books, although how he intended to repair the damaged tomes he didn't say.

'That doesn't leave much of a haul,' noted one of the men from the fyrd. 'But with that longship as a prize, we should all do well enough from this.'

Others heard him and readily agreed.

'Aye, although we never seem to get as much as we should,' mused one of them. 'By the time we've returned what belongs to the church, Lord AEthelred has taken his share and Wulfric and the guards from the Vill have claimed theirs, ours will be a miserly portion, although I grant you it's better than nothing. We've all of us been on missions such as this and come back with nothing to show for it except our wounds.' No one mentioned that most of them had seized personal plunder from those they'd killed as, strictly speaking, that should have been shared as well.

We were then offered food and the chance to make camp for the night. Most of us were grateful for that and for the warmth of a good fire but some of the men excused themselves and went instead into what remained of the ruined Minster to offer prayers to the good Lord to thank Him for having spared them.

* * *

As we started out early the next day, we had use of all the horses and the cart, but most of the mounted guards decided to let some of the wounded ride whilst they walked with the men or helped with the litters on which our dead were being carried. We therefore made slow progress and didn't reach the Vill until it was late. The men were told to make camp just outside the stockade where Lord AEthelred had arranged for a wild boar to be roasted on a spit over an open fire and provided ale for us all to celebrate our great victory. Wulfric and the Vill guards returned to the Hall and I was surprised when my father, Seth and myself were all invited to join them.

There was plenty of drinking in the Hall as well, although I noticed that my father was not inclined to partake of it, preferring instead to keep his own company even though he seemed to know several of the men who were there.

I was standing a little way apart from him when I noticed Edwina. It was not fitting for a lady of her status to remain in the Hall with the men so she turned and left. Glad to see her again, I followed her and found her waiting for me outside.

'So, you've returned,' she said. 'And by the looks of it you're none the worse for having endured your first battle.'

I just smiled, not quite sure what I should say given who she was.

'From what I hear of it, you were also something of a hero,' she teased.

'I didn't play much part in the actual fighting,' I admitted. 'I didn't even kill a single Viking but, as you can see, I did manage to rescue my father.'

She smiled. 'Well, it seems that my father is well pleased with what you all achieved. He also said that it was you who had the foresight to form the plan which led to our victory, thus I'm very proud of you.'

I looked away shyly, not quite sure what she meant by that. 'It was just an idea which came to me,' I said.

With that she leaned across and kissed me lightly on the cheek then walked away, stopping only to look back at me and smile as she had done the last time we met.

'So, what was that all about?' teased my father who had watched me leave the Hall and followed me. 'We leave you alone for a few days and you not only get yourself involved in one hell of a fight, but also go chasing after a girl as well!'

'It's not like that…' I protested.

'Oh, so what is it like?' he pressed, still teasing me.

Of course I couldn't answer. 'We spoke the other night,' I explained. 'She's Lord AEthelred's daughter.'

My father looked at me. 'That's Edwina?' he asked. 'She was but a child when I last heard tell of her!'

Seth, who had also joined us, then laughed. 'Well, she's not a child now. Nor I think is young Oscar. Although I dread to think what Lord AEthelred would say if he found out that you're trying to consort with his precious daughter!'

* * *

At some point before we all retired for the night, Lord AEthelred sent word asking me to join him in one of the smaller side rooms he kept for private meetings. At first, Seth's words rang in my ears and I began to think I would be severely chastised for showing any interest in Edwina who was surely far above my station. However, what he wanted was an entirely different matter altogether.

'You showed great insight in forming your plan of how to defeat the raiders and I would hear more of how that came about,' he said, inviting me to sit at the small table with him.

'My Lord, the idea just came to me,' I explained, feeling uncomfortable at sitting in his presence.

'What? From nowhere? Think back on it, lad. What gave you the idea in the first place?'

'My Lord, it was Wulfric who realised that they would need to reach their ship if they were to use it to carry off their plunder, so a shield wall placed between them and that objective seemed obvious. I remembered him saying that whilst both sides were well matched in terms of numbers, they would all be experienced warriors and the only way I could see for us to redress that would be to use the prisoners against them. After all, they all had a score to settle with the raiders and their number included skilled warriors like my father.'

He listened carefully. 'And you deduced all this even though you have never fought in a battle before?'

'Yes, my Lord. But then my father has told me many tales of the battles in which he fought so I could almost foretell what would happen at each stage of the fray. Thankfully, Wulfric managed to quickly form our shield wall after I'd been taken and...'

'But it was you who came up with the idea of using the prisoners, was it not?'

'Yes my Lord, albeit Wulfric refined my plan.'

'Even so, such insight is a rare gift. I've known others who have a similar ability but they were all experienced warriors.' With that he leaned back in his chair as if to consider matters.

'My Lord, it was only my thoughts, nothing more.'

'Oh, it's a lot more than that. You seem to have a skill which I could well use given the troubled times in which we live. We'll speak more about that tomorrow. In the meantime, you have my thanks for your part in securing a victory none of us believed we could ever hope to achieve.'

MY SHARE OF THE SPOILS

The next morning, all the members of the fyrd who had taken part in the battle came into the Hall eager to collect their due. Having set aside that which was to be returned to the Church, what remained of the spoil had been laid out on a trestle. It included some jewellery and other items but, as expected, there was little of significant value. Beside it, Lord Athelred had placed a small chest which contained a number of silver coins.

'You have all done us proud,' announced Lord AEthelred loud enough for all to hear. 'From what Wulfric has reported, it would seem that these raiders could well be part of the Viking army which is now rampant in all the lands north of here, thus you did well to defeat them. Your courage and battle skills remind me of how Saxons used to fight. Unfortunately, as you can see, there was little of substantial value recovered from the raiders except their longship and even that must be given over to one of the coastal settlements and used to fight off any raiders even before they reach our shores. That should be of benefit to us all in due course but it means there's nothing which can be readily divided for distribution.'

Even as he said it, I could feel the disappointment from everyone in the Hall. Undeterred by that, Lord AEthelred continued.

'I therefore propose to reward each of you with hard coin.'

At that, the mood improved immediately, particularly when the men who had served in the fyrd were called up to file past the trestle. As they did so, they were told they could each take a coin from the chest plus several were also awarded an additional coin to reflect their experience or the part they'd played in the battle. In the end, all seemed to agree that Lord AEthelred had been more than generous, particularly given that most men had secretly secured some personal plunder already. The prisoners who had been released were not included as being set free and thereby escaping slavery was considered to be reward enough, but some coins were set aside for the families of those who had died and also for the wounded who had remained under the care of the monks. When that was done the men were thanked by Lord AEthelred then given ale before being released from their service and allowed to return to their homes.

As usual, the Vill guards were given their reward separately, including a share which was set aside for those who had been left with the captured ship. All seemed well satisfied with that. Then my father was invited to approach Lord AEthelred. As he did so, I noticed that whilst remaining respectful, he didn't kneel before his Lord as I'd been made to do. Instead, he stood with his head bowed and waited for him to speak.

'I'm pleased to see you safely returned from your ordeal,' said Lord AEthelred.

'Thank you, my Lord. I'm grateful for your efforts to free me.'

'Don't thank me,' said Lord AEthelred. 'It's your son who persuaded us to that course. More than that, I gather from Wulfric that it was he who came up with the plan to defeat the raiders.'

At that, all eyes were looking at me. I wasn't quite sure what was expected of me but, in the end, I was beckoned forward by Wulfric who persuaded me to join my father. As I knelt beside him, I was suddenly aware that Lord AEthelred was laughing. 'Oscar, you may also remain standing, for you've surely earned that right.'

As I got to my feet, I had no idea what was going to happen next. Fortunately, it was Lord AEthelred who spoke again.

'I intend that you and your father shall both be well rewarded for the parts you each played. Oswald, for leading the prisoners you are invited to take two coins from the chest. I shall also send two men from the fyrd – a carpenter and a forester, to help you rebuild your farmstead at my expense. Hopefully that will mean you can restore your home more quickly.'

My father thanked him for that.

'That just leaves the question of what we should do with young Oscar here,' continued Lord AEthelred. 'In my view, he should receive three coins to reflect his pluck, his quick thinking and his courage.'

That represented a very significant sum so, feeling pleased with myself, I thanked him.

'There's more,' continued Lord AEthelred. 'The ability to see a strategy in battle to supplement our usual tactics of a shield wall is a rare gift and one which I will surely need if an invasion of Wessex is indeed imminent as Wulfric now fears it is.'

'Is that because of the longship we found, my Lord?' I asked.

'We're not yet sure. It could herald the start of the invasion or may simply mean that raids are likely to become more frequent. Either way, I would have you remain here at the Vill where you will have the chance to develop your skills and eventually become one of my military advisers.'

I wasn't sure what to say. 'My Lord, that's indeed a great honour but I surely don't deserve it after just one success.'

'Agreed. One swallow does not a summer make, but I sense you have something about you. We'll also teach you the rudiments of battle, although I suspect your father will want to resist that.' Even as he spoke, he looked to my father, thereby inviting him to reply.

'He is very young my Lord,' he protested.

'Aye, that he is. And so much the better for he can hardly have learned any bad habits which need to be resolved. Besides, I see something of you in this boy.'

'You know my views on him becoming a warrior, my Lord,' was all my father said.

'I do,' acknowledged Lord AEthelred. 'But we must all of us stand together against these raids and play what part we can.'

'I didn't raise him to see him slaughtered in the shield wall, my Lord. I did my share of that and no good ever came from spilling so much blood.'

Lord AEthelred seemed to accept that. 'Be that as it may, I'm obliged to use what skills and resources I have at my disposal. You'll be pleased to know that whilst he will need to learn how to fight, he won't be required to serve in the shield wall. His job will be to help me devise ways in which to drive off any raiders or, better still, defeat them. That's every bit as important as fighting; perhaps even more so. As such, I shall call him "Oscar the battle planner" from now on.'

Everyone still present laughed although I wasn't sure that Lord AEthelred meant it in jest. When the others realised he was serious, a cheer went up instead.

I was unsure how I felt about my new role and my father was clearly ill at ease with it, although he seemed to accept that he had no choice but to agree. 'Very well my Lord,' he said. 'Then I trust he'll serve you well.'

'Ah! He'll serve us well enough,' mused Lord AEthelred, smiling. 'Make no mistake about that. He's already shown that he has the guts for battle and also has a good head on his shoulders. I'm sure we can expect great things from him, particularly as he has the blood of a fine warrior in his veins.'

* * *

Later, when I stood with my father as he prepared to return home, he actually embraced me. It was the first time I ever recall him doing that.

'Oscar, I would much prefer that you were coming home with Seth and me,' he said. 'But it seems you have important work to do. As you know, I had hoped to spare you what I went through whilst serving in the guard but that's no longer up to me. The path you must now follow has been determined by others, even if it's not one I would have chosen for you. All I can advise is that you now serve Lord AEthelred as best you may.'

'Don't worry,' said Wulfric. 'I'll keep an eye on him. I owe you that much and more from when you saved my life all those years ago.'

My father looked relieved to hear that, then turned to speak to me again. 'Both I and your mother will pray that the Good Lord in his mercy will see you return to us safe and sound.' With that he took his sword and handed it to me. 'I think you'll have more use for this than I will. As you know, it once belonged to my father who also wielded it with great pride in the service of the Saxon cause.'

I took the sword and proudly examined it, then kissed the hilt of it as a sign of my respect and reverence for what I knew was an important part of my family's heritage.

'You'll need to have it blessed,' advised Wulfric. 'For it was used against us in the battle so there could well be Saxon blood on the blade.'

I acknowledged that then thanked my father.

'You have made me very proud,' he whispered as he embraced me yet again. 'For is it not the wish of every man that his son will achieve more in life than he did?'

Even as he spoke, I could feel his tears damp on my cheek. Wulfric must have seen them too.

'Don't worry,' he said. 'Oscar will be safe enough with us, be assured of that. He has to find his own place in this world as have we all and there's nothing you can say or do that will change that.'

THE SHADOW OF WAR LOOMS OVER US

After several weeks at the Vill, I was permitted to return to my parents for Yuletide where I helped them to finish rebuilding their farmstead. It was a somewhat difficult time for me, not least because my father seemed still to resent my being taken to serve with the Vill guard even though I would not actually be fighting. In the end, I received word that I was obliged to return to my duties, so left my family and walked back to Fordingwic before following the narrow path beside the river which I'd used before. Even as I approached the Vill, I could tell that all was not well. The gates were firmly shut and there were armed men on the ramparts. As I entered the Vill compound, I found Rufus waiting there to greet me.

'What's happening?' I asked.

'Have you not heard?'

'Heard what?'

He took me aside so that we could speak in private. 'Chippenham has fallen,' he said, his voice laden with concern. 'There was a surprise attack in which King Alfred was routed. It's not yet clear whether he was killed or managed to flee abroad but either way, Jarl Guthrum has the Vill there and is now poised to take over the whole of Wessex.'

I stared at him, trying to take in what he was saying. At first, words simply wouldn't come to express all the fearful thoughts which were tumbling around in my head.

'Lord AEthelred would have everyone attend him,' continued Rufus. 'I was told to take you to the Hall as soon as you arrive. Even now he's speaking with many of the thanes and nobles who have come from all corners of the Shire.'

Still reeling from the news, I went with Rufus to the main chamber. There we found about thirty senior thanes all seated around an extended trestle with Lord AEthelred at their head. We joined the many people who were standing at the back, all listening to a man named Osric. I didn't know Osric except that he was a very senior thane who held various estates within the Shire.

'How can this have happened?' he continued, sounding incredulous. 'We expect raids in the middle of winter, but never a full-scale invasion at this time of the year!'

'That's the trouble,' replied one of the others. 'These heathens don't abide by the normal rules of war.'

'Not so,' warned Bishop Leonfric, his reedy voice ringing out above the murmurs of all the others. 'Surely the attack by these heathens is a sign from God. He's reminding us that we need to mend our ways, having become lax in our worship of late.'

Lord AEthelred listened carefully but, in the end, it seemed he'd heard enough. 'We don't yet know what happened at Chippenham,' he reminded us. 'We'll get word soon enough but for now we must assume the worst - that Alfred is slain or has fled and that his army has been defeated. If that's true, then Guthrum will seek to conquer and secure the realm of Wessex for himself and, to do that, he'll need to clear away any pockets of armed resistance such as this.'

'Surely they'll not make their move until the weather improves?' suggested one man.

Lord AEthelred quickly dismissed that point. 'The weather won't save us. Many of these heathen Vikings come from lands much colder than ours so won't be easily deterred by that. We must assume the worst and prepare ourselves accordingly.'

'Will you not lead us, my Lord? The people would surely follow you if you did,' suggested Osric.

Others seemed to agree with Osric but Lord AEthelred looked shocked. 'What, would you have me usurp Lord Alfred as our King!'

'No my Lord,' said Osric. 'But if Alfred has indeed been slain, would you not be the obvious man to take his place?'

It was clear to us all that what Osric really wanted was for his Lord to assume the throne of Wessex and thereby enhance his own position. Not surprisingly, Lord AEthelred saw through that at once. 'That would be a decision for the Witan and would require the support of every Ealdorman in Wessex,' he said firmly. 'But there are better men than I to assume overall command.'

'Not so, my Lord. Are you not of Alfred's blood?' countered Osric.

Lord AEthelred considered that before he answered. 'I am his cousin by birth but there are others who have more of Alfred's blood in their veins than I do.'

'You mean Alfred's nephew, Aethelwold, my Lord? He could well take his turn to rule in the course of time but is as yet too young. What we need now is an experienced warrior to lead us. If that troubles you, why not step up and defeat Guthrum then hand the throne to Aethelwold when he's of age? God willing, by then we'll live in more settled times but, for now, only you have the battle skills and experience which are needed.'

'No!' stressed Lord AEthelred. 'I'll not raise an army whilst there's any chance that Alfred still lives. To do so could split our limited resources which would then make it impossible for him to strike back if and when he can. That's my final word on the matter.'

'If he still lives, my Lord.'

'Aye, if he still lives. But that's a decision we can make only once we know more. In the meantime, return to your lands and muster all your men to defend themselves and their homes. That is the duty of every able Saxon. So, raise arms and erect what defences you may. If Guthrum would take this land from us he must be made to pay for it with the blood of his warriors.'

'Surely, my Lord, we should offer a combined force to meet him in battle, even if led by you in Alfred's name?'

Lord AEthelred turned to me. 'Oscar, what say you?'

With that a murmur passed through the assembled nobles.

'What, do you fear to hear what young Oscar has to say?' pressed Lord AEthelred.

'Not fear my Lord,' replied Osric. 'But what can he know of such matters, he's but a boy?'

'Perhaps. But I urge you to listen, for this "boy" has an insight into such matters and I would hear him.'

With that they were silenced so I stepped forward and hurriedly considered how best to answer.

'My Lord, I agree with you,' I found myself saying. 'If you assemble an army it will give Guthrum a single target. He has only to defeat that army in battle and all Wessex would be his for the taking. On the other hand, if you assemble pockets of resistance, he will be obliged to split his force and tackle them one by one. That and the weather will delay him and perhaps give Lord Alfred time to strike back.'

No one spoke until Lord AEthelred broke the silence. 'What if any of these pockets of resistance are defeated?' he asked.

'Then they will have to decide whether to die or to live under Guthrum's rule, my Lord; a decision I fear we may all of us have to face sooner or later. Better still, they could retreat to add their numbers to other groups, thereby strengthening them. If so, they should leave nothing the invaders can use in terms of food and provisions – having to scavenge for what they need as they advance will delay them still further.'

I could tell that what I'd said had made sense to most of the men there. Even Lord AEthelred nodded as if to acknowledge that. 'So,' he said firmly. 'You have my decision. Return to your lands and make ready to defend them. I shall send word to the other Ealdormen of Wessex and suggest they follow my lead on this. Then, once we know what has become of our beloved King, we can decide how best to proceed.'

THE PROSPECT OF BATTLE

As the thanes left and returned to their homes and settlements, Lord AEthelred had Rufus, Wulfric and myself attend him in one of his private chambers.

'So,' he said. 'What have we do?'

It was Wulfric who answered. 'My Lord, this place is as good as any from which to make our stand. For that, we must allow the people who reside here to leave the settlement and seek sanctuary where they may. That should help to reduce civilian casualties but the members of the fyrd who reside within one hour's march of here must be summoned. Also, all those who work here at the Vill, including all servants, must be ordered to remain. That should ensure that we have an adequate force with which to defend this place.'

'How many men would that give us?' asked Lord AEthelred.

Wulfric did some hurried calculations before answering. 'By my reckoning, my Lord, that should give us a force of about one hundred men who are able to fight. But we must first strengthen our defences as some parts of the stockade are in need of repair.'

'Then see to it,' ordered Lord AEthelred bluntly. 'Also, send someone to keep watch in Fordingwic so they can warn us if and when Guthrum's men are sighted.' He then turned his attention to some domestic arrangements for which he summoned his Reeve. 'I would have you check the well as we may not be able to access the river to get fresh water if this does become a siege. Also, oversee the stockpiling of food and firewood and set the women to making a goodly supply of arrows before they leave.'

It was the first time the word 'siege' had been mentioned. A siege was something we all dreaded as it usually meant being starved until we surrendered – after which we would all be slaughtered anyway.

At that he paused as if to consider what else needed to be done. 'Rufus,' he continued, 'I want you to organise hunting trips to stock our larder. Find deer and wild boar and anything else which will feed us. Take two men with you to act as your bearers to carry back what you kill.' With that he rose and left the chamber, clearly no happier about our position than were the rest of us.

* * *

The Vill quickly became a hive of industry. What with people preparing to leave and others arriving, not to mention those who were to remain setting about whatever tasks had been assigned to them, it was difficult to know exactly what was going on at any one time. Amid so much turmoil I had been overlooked and hadn't been assigned to any particular role.

'Have you ever been hunting?' asked Wulfric when I mentioned that to him.

'Only for birds, sir. I can bring them down with my sling,' I told him.

'Pah! Birds won't suffice with so many mouths to feed. We need bigger game and plenty of it if we're to hold out here for any length of time. Go with Rufus and he'll teach you how to hunt and perhaps show you how to shoot a bow. That skill would serve you well if and when we are attacked.'

I quickly found Rufus who, having selected two burly men to act as his bearers, was already preparing to leave. He didn't seem overly impressed when I explained what Wulfric had suggested.

'It takes years to master the art of shooting a bow,' he complained. 'Not only that, but your arm will need to become used to the effort needed to draw it back far enough for the arrow to have any effect. What the hell does he expect me to teach you in a few hunting trips!'

Even so, he agreed that I could go with them so the four of us set off from the Vill and made our way to the forest. Once there, Rufus stressed how important it was to move quietly so as not to disturb our quarry. With that in mind, we followed him for some time, creeping through the trees and foliage until Rufus found the trail of a deer. How he could do that I couldn't say, he just seemed to know which way a deer had passed and was then able to follow it. Eventually he ordered us all to get down low as he could see his potential target in a clearing ahead of us.

'Stay here,' he whispered. 'Don't move and don't make so much as a sound.' With that he slipped away on his own, working his way around the deer so as to get downwind of it. I couldn't resist looking and was surprised to see a fine stag which, although a long way off, Rufus clearly regarded it as being within his range.

I fear the stag must have seen me or somehow sensed our presence but, as it began to move off, Rufus was too quick for it. He loosed his arrow, striking the poor beast in the hindquarters. It was not enough to bring the animal down and it bounded off into the undergrowth. Rufus was up and after it at once, as were the others so I followed and pretty soon we found the injured animal all but exhausted. As such it was a sitting target and Rufus had one of the men dispatch it with a spear.

Having examined the kill, the two bearers tied its legs to a stout pole then lifted that onto their shoulders.

'Is one enough?' I asked.

'It'll have to be,' laughed Rufus. 'Unless you're minded to carry the next one back on your own.'

* * *

Once back at the Vill, I was once more summoned to see Lord AEthelred in one of the small private chambers. I found him sitting with Wulfric at a table, both of them looking very forlorn.

'You wanted to see me, my Lord?' I questioned as I entered.

He looked up at me and managed a sort of smile. 'Yes Oscar. We need to discuss what best to do when the Vikings eventually reach us.'

'My Lord, how long have we got before they get here?' I asked.

He shrugged. 'Who can say? Guthrum will want to secure Wessex as quickly as he can, but how long that will take depends on the weather and on how much resistance his men encounter.'

'Do you think that gives us a few weeks, my Lord?'

'A few weeks? Yes, probably at least that. We'll know more once word about what happened at Chippenham reaches us but, assuming what we've learned so far is true, this and other important settlements will be among his first targets. Once he's taken them, the rest of Wessex will fall easily enough.'

'Will he lead these attacks himself?' I asked.

'I doubt it,' said Wulfric. 'More likely he'll leave that to his senior Jarls.'

'Then what should we expect in terms of numbers?'

Again, it was Wulfric who answered. 'A sizeable force, that's for certain. They'll most likely send out small warbands to intimidate the smaller settlements and thereby subdue them. The larger settlements such as this they'll seek to take by sheer force of numbers.'

'So, my Lord, what will happen if this does become a siege?' I asked.

'They'll either try to batter down the gates and force their way into the Vill or try to starve us out,' said Wulfric.

That was all much as I feared. 'Will the weather not help us?' I asked. 'If it snows, as Rufus thinks it will, that should at least slow them up and thereby give Alfred time to strike back.'

They both considered that for a moment. 'That's assuming

Alfred is still alive and has anything resembling an army with which to do so,' Lord AEthelred pointed out.

'Then, my Lord, there's nothing more we can do for now,' I suggested. 'Once we know what we're up against we may be able to do more.'

He looked at me almost dolefully as though he was already feeling the heavy burden of command. 'Whatever we do, the toll of those who are slain is likely to be high. And I fear there's nothing I can do to counter that.'

WE PREPARE OUR DEFENCES

I didn't go hunting with Rufus again after that but I did manage to catch a few fish from the river which we then smoked so they would keep if properly stored.

Apart from that, during the next few weeks all continued in much the same way. Men arrived from various parts of the Shire intent on joining us whilst those who were allowed to leave the settlement were preparing to do so or had already left. Strangely, no one seemed concerned about using or even protecting the newly vacated homes in the settlement as almost everyone preferred to shelter within the safety of the Vill itself.

It was during this time that I was shown how to wield a sword and, whilst nowhere near proficient, I did manage to get the way of handling that and other weapons. However, my instruction and practise was interrupted when it began to snow and everyone relaxed knowing that it was unlikely Guthrum would attack in such bad weather. Despite the snow, work on the defences continued, albeit slowly, and others took to hunting as the snow made it easier for those less skilled than Rufus to track and stalk their prey. Apart from that, all we could do was wait.

During that time, Edwina and I met quite often, although as friends rather than as anything more. Nonetheless, we were both of us concerned lest her father should see us together and then forbid us from meeting. That worried me, not just because there were by then no others of about my age left in the settlement, but also because I realised that we were gradually growing much closer.

Despite the threat of the attack which still hung over us, Lord AEthelred organised a modest feast which was intended to lift the men's spirits and was welcomed by all. Soon after that, a man arrived with news of what was going on elsewhere within the realm.

The messenger introduced himself as Aelwyn. He was a thane who claimed to have been with Alfred at Chippenham so had witnessed the events there at first hand. We gave him food and made him welcome, all the time anxious to hear what news he had to impart.

'From what we know, Jarl Guthrum split from the forces which were invading Mercia,' he told us as we all listened intently, hanging on his every word. 'He marched on Chippenham with a sizeable army and struck under the cover of night, thereby taking us by surprise whilst we were celebrating Christmas. We none of us expected them to attack in the midst of winter and, after a hard year of campaigning, many members of Alfred's army had returned to their homes and families, thus his forces were woefully under strength.'

'Even so, how on earth did they breach the defences?' demanded Lord AEthelred.

Aelwyn was slow to answer as if choosing his words with care. 'My Lord, I fear we may have been betrayed. Perhaps someone opened the gates, for the Viking army poured through them, wreaking havoc and slaughter. The Saxons fought well but many good men died.'

'Betrayed!' queried Lord AEthelred angrily. 'Who would do such a thing?'

Still Aelwyn was slow to answer. 'My Lord, it's rumoured that several men of noble birth took it upon themselves to betray Alfred to the Vikings. By doing so, they hoped to end all these years of hostilities and bring peace to the realm, albeit under Guthrum's rule.'

We were all of us stunned into silence by that.

'Looking to help themselves more likely!' accused Lord AEthelred. 'Can you name these traitors?'

'No, my Lord. It is, as I said, but a rumour.'

'What then of Alfred? Was he among the fallen?'

'No my Lord. He and his family managed to escape and are now in hiding. I can't say where because I don't know. It's said that he and a few loyal followers have found somewhere safe to see out the winter.'

'A few loyal followers!' noted Lord AEthelred angrily. 'What good is that to our cause?'

Aelwyn smiled. 'Don't worry my Lord. All is not yet lost. I and others were despatched by Alfred to ensure that people like you hold themselves ready for when he does strike back. He's beaten for now, but remember, once cornered in his lair, a lion will always come out fighting. Hence you must be ready for his return.'

'And what do we do in the meantime?'

'My Lord, when I left Chippenham, Guthrum was already sending out war bands seeking to establish control of all Wessex.'

'Which is as we feared! And no doubt they're killing and thieving as they go!'

'Not so, my Lord. They steal food and supplies with which to feed themselves but Guthrum seems to want to leave as much in place within the realm as he can. After all, he'll need to raise taxes to pay his army so will be hoping for as little resistance from the ordinary people as possible, all of whom will be forced to accept him as their Lord.'

'They'll never do that!' Lord AEthelred assured us.

'I fear they will, my Lord. For most people it matters not who they serve. They'll pay what's due to whoever demands it – particularly those who hold a sword to their throats.'

Again there was silence

'So how long before Guthrum's men reach us here?' asked Lord AEthelred, posing the question we all of us wanted to ask.

Aelwyn shrugged. 'Two or three weeks at best, my Lord. Once they've taken this place they'll then move on to Winchester which will be of more strategic value to them. For that they'll need to have their forces intact. That's your best chance, for they won't want to be delayed here for too long - nor will they want to risk their men being slain as they'll need all the warriors they can muster.'

'We're already well prepared for that and will give a good account of ourselves,' boasted Lord AEthelred, seeming somewhat calmer and more inclined to listen to what Aelwyn had to tell us.

Aelwyn looked at him as if he knew that was just a hollow boast rather than a realistic proposition. 'My Lord, you'll be facing an army of fearsome Viking warriors. How long do you expect to hold out against them?'

'As long as it takes,' answered Lord AEthelred proudly. 'As you've said, they can't afford to wait at our gates for long, particularly in this weather. They'll all freeze to death if they do!' He then looked to me. 'What say you, Oscar?'

I'd been thinking hard about what had been said and already concluded that what Aelwyn was trying to say was right. 'We'll do our best, my Lord,' I said as tactfully as I could. 'That or we'll all die trying.'

* * *

Aelwyn left the next day to visit other settlements which might be able to support Alfred if and when he did strike back. No sooner had he left than Lord AEthelred ordered myself and Wulfric to attend him.

'So Oscar, what did you make of it all?' he asked.

'Do you mean about Alfred having been betrayed my Lord?' I asked hoping to avoid having to answer that particular question.

'No,' snapped Lord AEthelred. 'The truth of that remains to be seen. But I sensed that you have doubts about our chances of holding out here for long.'

'My Lord, given that they mean to conquer the whole of Wessex,

I agree with you, they'll want to breach our defences here as quickly as they can and then move on.'

'Exactly. And we should be well placed to delay them with all we've put in hand.'

'We could also slow them down before they get here, my Lord.'

'What do you mean?'

'Simply that we could go out to meet them. Not in force, you understand, but a few men could do a lot to impede them as they march towards us.'

Lord AEthelred looked to be intrigued. 'In what way?' he asked.

'They'll likely choose the most direct route to get here which will mean following the narrow track from Fordingwic which runs beside the river. Therefore, if our bowmen were to take up positions within the trees on the opposite bank, we should be able to kill a few of them before they reach us here.'

Both Wulfric and Lord AEthelred seemed to like my idea. 'Now that's what I call good thinking!' announced the Ealdorman. 'Let's give them a taste of what they can expect from Saxon warriors! Hopefully we can then delay them here until such time as Alfred is ready to make his glorious return.'

COMETH THE HOUR, COMETH THE FOE

The snow was the heaviest fall we'd seen for many years, blown into deep drifts by a sharp wind from the north. It remained just about possible for people to travel, but Guthrum could have no hope of conquering the whole of Wessex in such foul weather. As it turned out, it was several weeks before the snow subsided and our thoughts once more turned to the prospect of an attack. Sure enough, within two weeks of that, word reached us that a large contingent of Vikings had been sighted marching towards Fordingwic and would therefore reach us in a matter of days. Lord AEthelred immediately summoned Wulfric, Rufus and myself to speak with him in the Hall. 'I'm told that it's a very large warband,' advised Lord AEthelred, sounding worried. 'So Oscar, I would hear more about the plan you mentioned.'

'As I explained, my Lord, as they approach via the path from Fordingwic, we'll need to position bowmen within the trees, keeping the river between them and us. The path is narrow on the far side so they should be in single file or, at worst, two abreast. The plan is not to kill them but to wound as many as we can.'

'Why not just kill the bastards and be done with it!' asked Wulfric.

'Because we want to slow their advance as much possible in order to buy time for us and possibly other settlements as well. They'll either bury their dead or leave them where they fall, whereas those we wound will need to be carried and tended. They'll also still need feeding which will deplete whatever limited resources of food they've brought with them.'

'Ha!' said Lord AEthelred. 'It's a good plan. Wulfric, how many men will you take with you?'

'I think just ten, my Lord. That should suffice and will still leave enough men here to defend the Vill just in case they slip past us using another track rather than the path beside the river.'

Lord AEthelred seemed satisfied with that. 'What about you Rufus? No doubt you'll now suspend your hunting parties with the enemy so close at hand?'

Rufus looked to Wulfric and myself before he answered as it was something the three of us had discussed already. It was Wulfric who answered for us all.

'My Lord, with your permission, I would like Rufus to come with us. He's without doubt our most skilled bowman and could serve us well if we get a chance to kill whoever is leading the warband. That would delay them even more.'

'Good. Then what about you, young Oscar? Where will you serve?'

'My Lord, if I could, I'd like to go with Wulfric as well. I won't add much to their numbers but it would help if I could assess the enemy's strength at first hand.'

Lord AEthelred agreed to that at once. 'Good, let's try to give these heathens a harsh welcome. I suggest you leave as soon as you're ready and take up a position whereby you can track them the whole way here, harrying them at every step.'

'My Lord, what about the footbridge across the river?' asked Wulfric. 'Should we not destroy that as well?'

Lord AEthelred considered that then dismissed it. 'No, there's no point. Even if we destroy it, they'll only wade across so we might as well leave it intact. At least we'll then know when and where they're crossing.'

* * *

By the next morning, Rufus had ensured that all the men who were to come with us had a bow and a quiver of arrows. We therefore set off at once, crossing the bridge then marching along the narrow path which we expected the Vikings to follow. After some time, we used a shallow riffle to cross back over the river then worked our way through the forest until we found the perfect spot for our ambush; a place where there was plenty of foliage we could use to conceal ourselves. All we had to do then was wait, trying to keep warm as best we could given that we dared not light a fire for fear of giving ourselves away. Fortunately, the Vikings appeared quite soon, a long line of them marching in single file along the path on the other side of the river, just as we expected.

'Everyone keep out of sight,' ordered Wulfric then turned to Rufus. 'We'll follow your lead and go on your command.'

Rufus made a hurried assessment of the situation. 'Right, when I give the word I would have you all loose the first flight of arrows at the same time, thereby taking them by surprise. After that, they'll raise their shields and it'll be the devil's own job to hit them. Our best chance is to then divide into two groups. The first will release their arrows into the air. They'll have no choice but cover themselves by holding their shields above their heads thereby leaving themselves exposed. When they do that, the second group should be able to hit a few more of the bastards. So, pick a target and wait on my command. I'll take the man at the front of the line as the chances are he'll be their leader or at least a man of some consequence. And remember, it's better to maim or wound them, we don't want to kill them all outright. At least, not yet.'

As the Vikings drew closer it was clear that they were indeed a formidable force. I counted their numbers as best I could and decided there was possibly two hundred men; thus as Lord AEthelred had said, a significant warband. What's more, all of them appeared to be well armed and were no doubt seasoned warriors. As we watched them, Rufus held his nerve until they were directly opposite us then stepped forward. 'Now!' he ordered and, with that, we each of us loosed an arrow.

At least eight of them fell to the first barrage. The others then quickly raised their shields, thereby making it very difficult for us to exact any further damage, just as Rufus had predicted.

'Right,' said Rufus. 'Every other man must now shoot into the air,' he bellowed, keeping to the plan.

We did as he ordered and sure enough, the Vikings raised their shields above their heads as the arrows clattered down upon them like hail. Almost at once the second volley was loosed aimed directly at those who were thereby exposed, striking at least half a dozen more of them. Unfortunately, being seasoned warriors, our ploy wouldn't work again as they hurriedly divided themselves into small groups, sharing the cover of their shields. Some of them also retreated into the forest behind them and even began to shoot back at us.

'Withdraw!' ordered Wulfric. 'We'll move further downstream and wait for them there.'

At that, we did as he ordered and faded back into the forest. Unfortunately, we found only two other places on our side of the river where we could repeat the assault in the same way and neither offered much in the way of cover.

'What do you think?' asked Rufus.

'I think it was a good ploy but it won't work as well again,' replied Wulfric. 'Besides, we can't afford to risk losing any men. Just knowing that we could be around every bend in the river will slow them up so we best serve our cause by now getting back to the Vill to support the defences there.'

'With your permission I'll stay,' said Rufus. 'I should be able to pick off a few more of them.'

'Very well, but just be careful. You know what happens if you're caught. We can't afford to lose you - and you can't afford to let yourself be taken – at least, not whilst still alive.'

* * *

All those at the Vill had been busy making ready for the assault. As we rejoined them, Wulfric thanked our small band then he and I went to make our report to Lord AEthelred.

'There must have been at least two hundred of them, my Lord,' said Wulfric. 'And all of them well armed.'

'I feared as much,' said Lord AEthelred. 'So Oscar, did your ploy work?'

'From what I could see we wounded perhaps a dozen or more and killed several others, my Lord. But after that they took shelter behind their shields.'

'My Lord, they could be upon us within the hour,' stressed Wulfric. 'Rufus has remained to keep them on their toes which should slow them down a bit, but that's about all we can hope for.'

Lord AEthelred looked to me. 'So, what do we do now?'

'My Lord, all we can do is give everyone here a bow and man the ramparts of the stockade. We have food, water and warmth enough for now, whereas they'll soon be cold and hungry. With luck we may be able to outlast them.'

Lord AEthelred turned away from us. 'I hate sieges!' he said aloud. 'They never turn out well!'

Wulfric seemed to agree. 'Besides, they won't want to wait around for long,' he warned. 'It's my guess that they'll charge the gates and break them down or, failing that, will set them ablaze. Once they've achieved that they'll swarm through the breach and we'll all be slain!'

'I can see no other option,' I said.

'There is one,' said Lord AEthelred. 'We hit them before they've had a chance to settle. We could charge out at first light tomorrow and kill as many as we can, thereby reducing their numbers. They won't be expecting that and it's therefore the best chance we have.'

I was horrified. 'Your guards might fare well enough during the assault but most of these men will be no match for battle hardened warriors, particularly when outnumbered by at least two to one!'

Wulfric looked at me. 'Can you suggest anything better?' he asked.

I had to admit I couldn't. 'No, but surely they won't have the wherewithal to break down the gates,' I reasoned. 'They'll be easy targets if they so much as try!'

But Lord AEthelred had already made his decision. 'The stockade should hold for a while,' he agreed. 'But once they get tired of waiting, they'll simply set it on fire then hack their way through the charred and blackened timbers. I've seen it happen before. We therefore have to strike first and take the fight to them. That's our best defence.'

I looked at Wulfric and could see that he was minded to agree. 'I think Lord AEthelred is right,' he said. 'If I'm going to die, I'd rather do so fighting like a true Saxon, not roasting amidst the flames waiting to be slaughtered.'

* * *

Having left the Hall, Wulfric and I went to see what was going on beyond the Vill. Many men were already gathered on the ramparts so we joined them and could see that a large contingent of warriors had already arrived and had made camp just beyond the gates, many of them occupying the deserted homes in the settlement. More still were crossing the footbridge and others were lining up along the far bank of the river waiting to join them.

'They're staying just beyond range,' said Rufus who had, by then, rejoined us. 'It seems they know what they're about.'

'They certainly have us outnumbered,' mused Wulfric.

'What does Lord AEthelred say?' asked Rufus.

'That we're to attack them,' replied Wulfric.

Rufus stared at him, not quite sure what to say. 'But that's utter madness!' he managed at last. 'There's far too many of them!'

'I agree,' I said ruefully. 'I told him we should try to hold out for as long as we can. They'll be cold and hungry before too long so

109

may give up and leave us be. Either that or, for all we know, Alfred may soon be ready to strike back.'

'I wish that were so,' answered Wulfric. 'But even if he is, it won't be in time to save us. All we can do is prepare to die as best we can. Now, help me to organise the men but keep your reservations to yourself. I need our men to believe that they have every chance of coming through this fray alive.'

With that we went down from the ramparts and he summoned everyone to attend him. Apart from Edwina who had elected to stay with her father, all the women and children had left by then so it amounted to about one hundred men if you include all the members of the Vill guard.

'Lord AEthelred has determined that we should attack them and thereby take them by surprise. I'll lead the way with the guards close behind. I want a dozen men on the ramparts with bows and a good supply of arrows. They'll be commanded by Rufus and will cover us and pick off the enemy where they can. The rest of you are to follow the guards. We'll strike once as hard and as fast as we can, then regroup and return here - so leave the gates open until all are safely back inside.'

There was silence at first as men considered the plan. Not surprisingly, none of them much liked it.

'Why not stay here?' asked one of them.

'Aye, surely we'll be safer if we remain within the fortifications?' said another.

Wulfric answered them quickly. 'Yes, until they burn the place down around us! Lord AEthelred has ordered us to take the fight to the enemy so, unless you think you know more about battles than he does, I suggest we do as he says.'

With that everyone was quiet as if trying to make sense of what had been said.

'I want everyone to assemble here at first light armed and wearing whatever war gear you have. Rufus will select those who are to man the ramparts. Remember, this is our best hope for surviving this attack and we all of us have our part to play.'

A FATAL ERROR

At first light the following morning, we all of us gathered at the Vill gates, shivering with the cold. The man who had been stationed on the ramparts overnight to keep watch reported that all was quiet and that so far as he could see, most of the Vikings were still sleeping. He couldn't account for those who had taken shelter in some of the deserted homes, but he was certain that if we attacked at once we would have the vital element of surprise.

Ever the warrior, Lord AEthelred decided to lead the charge himself and thereby set an example to us all. He walked through the assembled men then turned to face us. 'Remember your forefathers,' he said, keeping his voice low so as not to wake the enemy. 'Make them proud and fight like Saxons should.' With that he signalled for the gates to be opened. As soon as they were, he raised his sword. 'Charge!' he bellowed and we all of us followed him into what had become a veritable nest of vipers.

The bowmen immediately began loosing arrows whilst we surged forward, giving the enemy no chance to form even a rudimentary defence. Many were killed where they lay or were cut down as they spilled out of the homes where they'd taken shelter for the night. At first it seemed that speed and surprise had indeed prevailed but it was not enough. A group of them formed up and held us back long enough for the rest of their number to join the fray.

Whilst our men fought hard, they were no match for trained and battle-hardened warriors. Some were cut down with an axe whilst others were slain by sword or spear. They fell thick and fast until even Lord AEthelred himself was separated and surrounded. He was quickly taken down by an arrow which lodged in his back and, as he fell, one of the Vikings stepped forward and brutally hacked off his head with a battle axe. To the cheers of his comrades, the Viking who'd slain him held up Lord AEthelred's head by the hair like some sort of trophy.

The Vill guards were all sworn to protect their Lord or to die trying. They did their best to fulfil that obligation, hoping to at least recover his body, but all were killed, adding their own bodies to the pile of those which already lay beside him.

I knew then that all was lost. Already men were fleeing rather than waiting to be slain and I determined to do the same. It was then that I saw Wulfric who was some way apart from the main fray, fighting with two men at once – both armed with spears. He was wearing a mail tabard which was joined at the sides by leather straps to allow him freedom of movement but which left a gap which could be easily exploited. Both men saw that chance and took it. As one of them drove his shield into Wulfric's face, the other one stabbed his spear point home. Wulfric groaned as he felt the pain then twisted as if to free himself but, instead, fell to the ground. As both men then towered above him, he must have known that death would follow.

Seeing what had happened, I raised my sword and rushed to help Wulfric but Rufus responded even faster than I did. Having left the relative safety of the Vill to join the battle, he went at once to Wulfric's aid, loosing two arrows in quick succession as he did so. Neither man had time to react and both soon lay dead beside our badly wounded friend.

'We have to get him away from here!' shouted Rufus, pushing past me. Together we then lifted Wulfric to his feet and half dragged, half carried him from the field. 'We can take him to the church,' I suggested, pointing to the small chapel which served both the settlement and the Vill and which looked to be intact.

Rufus refused. 'No, they'll have already looted that hoping to find it stuffed full of silver. Some of them may still be there so we'll take him to that barn over there instead.'

At that stage the wound to Wulfric's side was bleeding freely and he seemed barely conscious as he groaned with pain. As soon as we reached the barn we laid him out on the floor and I used his cloak to try to staunch the flow of blood.

'The wound needs to be cauterised,' said Rufus. 'That will seal it and should ensure that it doesn't become infected.'

'Then let's do it!' I urged.

'No, not here, for it'll mean lighting a fire. If we can make it to the forest we can do it there as we should then be safe enough.'

By that time, most of our warriors were trying to flee but the Vikings were busy killing those they caught and putting our wounded to the sword. We watched in horror but could do nothing to stop the slaughter. At one point, several of them hoisted Lord AEthelred's headless body up onto a makeshift gantry then, laughing and jeering, they used it as a target for shooting arrows. Both Rufus and I were appalled, for although AEthelred had brought it all upon himself by not heeding my advice, he was a fair man, perhaps more so than most nobles and therefore deserved better than have his body treated thus. Then, when they'd finished with him, they began to toy with the bodies of the other men who had fallen, treating our dead with such contempt as to lewdly despoil their remains.

Once they'd finished their games, they turned their attention to the Vill itself which, with the gates still wide open as we'd arranged, was theirs for the taking. The few men who had remained inside the Vill hurriedly tried to close them again but were too late and the Vikings began to pour through into the Vill compound. We could only imagine what wanton damage they would do, though Rufus was certain that they would leave the buildings intact to use themselves.

'We should go whilst they're all busy with that,' suggested Rufus.

I knew he was right but was more concerned for the plight of Edwina than for myself. Of course, there was nothing I could do to help her so, instead, I did what I could for Wulfric who was still in considerable pain and weak from the loss of so much blood.

'We'll carry him between us,' suggested Rufus. With that, we lifted him up and, praying that no one would see us, hurried towards the trees. Once there we rested for a few moments before venturing deeper into the forest until we found a small clearing beside a stream where we felt we would be safe enough.

Rufus hurriedly lit a fire then took a knife from his belt and placed the blade in the flames. That done, I removed Wulfric's mail vest and his woollen undershirt so that Rufus could properly examine his wound. As I did so, I was shocked to see that his body was marred with many battle scars, including one which I took to be from an arrow which had lodged so close to his heart that I was surprised he'd survived it.

'The wound's deep but it's not too wide,' pronounced Rufus as he examined Wulfric's side. 'We'll cauterise it and hopefully it will then heal, albeit that will take time.'

As we waited for the blade to get hot enough, he urged me to wash the wound then tear off a strip from Wulfric's cloak to form a strop. Having done so, Rufus lifted the knife from the fire and held up the smoking blade whilst I pushed the strop between Wulfric's teeth.

'Right, hold him as firmly as you can,' urged Rufus. 'He'll twist and turn as I apply this to the wound but thank God he's barely conscious so won't feel the worst of it.' With that he pressed the still red hot blade against Wulfric's side.

He was right that Wulfric didn't feel the worst of it, but he still stiffened and grimaced as the blade was laid against his flesh. The strop prevented him from crying out as Rufus held the knife in place and, when it was done, Wulfric fell back, exhausted and unconscious. We then left him to find what comfort he could in that.

A TIME AND PLACE TO LICK OUR WOUNDS

'What's happened?' asked Wulfric as he at last regained consciousness.

By then we had established our camp in the clearing and Rufus had gone off to hunt for food. Wulfric was still in a great deal of pain and seemed to recall nothing of how the battle had ended.

'I fear we were routed,' I told him as I offered him some water taken from the nearby stream. 'Most of our men are dead or have fled the field.'

'Defeated!' he said, struggling to get up. As he did so he felt the pain in his side and so lay back down again.

'You were stabbed with a spear,' I reminded him. 'Rufus has cauterised the wound but you lost a lot of blood which is why you feel so weak.'

'What then of Lord AEthelred?' he pressed, more concerned with that than for his own predicament.

'I'm afraid he's dead,' I told him. 'He was taken down with an arrow then beheaded on the field. His guards couldn't reach him in time but all died trying.'

Wulfric stared at me in disbelief. 'Then what the hell am I doing here? I should lay with them for we were all of us sworn to die beside our Lord!'

'What good would that do now?' asked Rufus who had just returned from hunting. 'Besides, you're in no fit state to do anything more at present.'

At that he seemed to relax. 'What's then to be done?' he asked.

'Nothing,' I advised him. 'The Vikings have the Vill and are still busy wreaking havoc there, so we've taken shelter here meaning to escape when we can.'

'Escape? Where to?'

I thought about that for a moment. 'We could go north to Chippenham to see whether we can find what's left of Alfred's army?' I suggested.

'He can't travel until his wound has mended,' advised Rufus firmly. 'It really needed to be sewn up but I've nothing with which to do it. Only time will tell if what I've done will suffice.'

'It'll heal,' said Wulfric. 'Don't tarry on my account.'

Rufus laughed. 'Don't worry, we won't. But we're all of us tired and are in no fit state to go anywhere as yet. We should be safe enough here for a while and, once they've finished looting the Vill, they'll move on to Winchester. That is, after all, likely to be their prime objective.'

* * *

We remained in the forest for several weeks in order to rest and to give Wulfric's wound every chance to heal. As we waited, we fashioned a crude shelter to keep out the worst of the weather and had a small fire burning at all times to keep us warm. Meanwhile, Rufus provided us with food, some of which he shot with his bow but most he caught in simple traps he made himself from small branches cut from a willow. I added to this by catching eels and an occasional fish from the stream, the latter by using nothing but my bare hands - a trick old Seth had taught me. After several weeks Rufus seemed pleased with the way Wulfric's wound was healing. The red hot knife had left it sore but there was no sign of any infection.

'Oscar, you seem very quiet,' said Wulfric one evening. 'Have you something on your mind?'

'You mean apart from wondering if we'll ever survive this place?' I said.

'Well, at least we're alive and have all we need for now.'

'Yes, but I was also thinking about Edwina and the others at the Vill,' I admitted. 'I worry about what became of them.'

Wulfric shrugged. 'None of them will have fared well,' he said bluntly. 'The Vikings are noted for their brutality. Any women there will have been ill used for certain and the men will have either been killed or taken for slaves. I'm sorry if that's not what you want to hear, but it is the way of it.'

As I considered that, it troubled me greatly to think of what my family might also have suffered, particularly my parents. If they'd been attacked my father would no doubt have given a good account of himself but they would have had little chance of surviving another raid. Hopefully he, my mother and Odelia had left to seek safety somewhere. There was no such hope for Edwina. I prayed she had been killed quickly and cleanly rather than be taken and abused for, having been so high born, she would have found it hard to endure that or, indeed, a life in slavery. When I explained that, Wulfric nodded knowingly.

'Aye, but there's nothing to be done,' he assured me. 'Just count yourself lucky to have survived.'

'As should you!' teased Rufus trying to lighten the mood. 'You left more blood on that field than most men had in their veins to start with!'

Wulfric seemed to appreciate the humour. 'Well, if you two idle wastrels had carried me away more quickly, I'd be fully recovered by now.'

We all laughed but in fact it was a point well made. Wulfric had indeed lost a lot of blood which had left him still weak. He was also downhearted for having failed in his sworn duty to protect his Lord and no longer felt himself to be the warrior he once was. All we could hope was that food and rest would eventually restore him.

'I think we should remain here for a few weeks more,' announced Rufus. 'We'll then do as Oscar has suggested and make our way to Chippenham. Along the way we may learn of how things are and hopefully find news of Alfred's army.'

'We'll need to travel very carefully,' I reminded them. 'There are likely to be Viking warbands everywhere, raiding and foraging for themselves. We're none of us in a fit state to engage them. After all, the only weapons we have are my sword and a bow.'

We all agreed that was our best course. At least in the forest we felt safe enough to light a fire for warmth and were certainly eating well thanks to Rufus. However, the truth of it was that we couldn't stay there forever and needed to know what was happening elsewhere within the realm; in particular, whether or not Alfred was indeed alive and in hiding or whether he'd been taken and killed, thereby ceding control to Jarl Guthrum. Thus one morning Wulfric announced that he was ready to travel.

Taking him at his word, we cleared away all signs of the camp as best we could, took what food we could carry then set off towards Chippenham.

WE GO IN SEARCH OF OUR KING

It would normally have taken just two or three days to reach Chippenham but, with Wulfric still struggling because of his wound, we allowed ourselves at least a week to get there. Our journey was not helped by the fact that several times we encountered bands of Vikings and therefore had to hide until they'd passed. Rufus was tempted to take on some of the smaller groups with his bow but Wulfric advised against it.

'It's best we leave no sign of having been here,' he suggested.

That did seem to make sense and besides, we were in no hurry. Then, after three days on the road, we chanced upon a small farmstead where a widow was busy tending a brazier outside her humble cottage. We introduced ourselves and, as was the Saxon way, she invited us to join her.

'So, what news is there of Alfred? We've heard tell that he's somewhere in the west and would join him,' said Wulfric as we each drank a bowl of hot broth. It was weak and watery fare but welcome nonetheless.

'We can none of us speak as to his whereabouts,' she told us, obviously wary of trusting strangers. 'Although word is that he's well and intends to strike back.'

'So how then do we find him?' I asked.

'You follows your nose, boy. If the good Lord means you to find King Alfred, he'll show you the way right enough.'

'But what about you?' said Rufus. 'Are you not worried about being attacked? We could stay awhile longer if that would be of some comfort to you.'

'I need no more comfort than what I already have,' she replied.

'My husband, God rest his soul, was among them that was killed at the battle near Ashdown. All I pray is that I'll soon join him wherever it is he's gone, be it heaven or hell.'

Wulfric told her that he had fought at Ashdown as well and confirmed that it had been a particularly bloody battle by any standards. 'Alfred claimed it as a rare and much needed Saxon victory,' he told us. 'Although given the number of men who died there, it can hardly rate as a triumph.'

Having ascertained that we were loyal Saxons, the widow allowed us to sit beside her fire for the night then gave us more broth in the morning. After that we asked for directions to Chippenham then left, leaving some of our provisions by way of thanks for her hospitality.

We hadn't gone far when Wulfric noticed that we were being followed. It was just a single man so we were not unduly worried, at least not until Rufus spotted two others hiding behind the trees beside the track a short way ahead of us. 'Best ready ourselves,' he warned, unslinging the bow from his shoulder.

'If they meant to kill us they'd have likely done so by now,' suggested Wulfric. 'So just keep walking but spread out across the road to keep a good distance between us.'

We did as he suggested and, sure enough, the men Rufus had seen both stepped out to bar our path. They looked so alike that I took them to be brothers; both tall with blue eyes and hair which was almost yellow. They looked to be Saxons rather than Vikings but could equally well have been traitors – or even common thieves.

'What do you want with us?' challenged Wulfric suspiciously.

'That depends on who you are and where you're going,' said one of them.

'Is that any concern of yours?' replied Wulfric.

'In these uncertain times, is it not every man's duty to question strangers they meet on the road?' the man retorted.

Wulfric wisely let that pass. 'Well then, friend, since you're clearly not Vikings we must all be on the same side. We're survivors from a battle near a place known as Fordingwic. We've not yet had our fill of fighting and are therefore on our way to find Lord Alfred that we might join whatever's left of his army.'

'Is that so?' asked the man.

'Aye, that's the way of it. Unless you have a problem with that?'

'Only that I wonder what Lord Alfred would want with the likes of you. You look like vagrants and are unarmed, save for him with that bow and the boy with a sword almost too heavy for him to wield. You'll not add much to his numbers, whoever you are.'

Wulfric rounded on him sharply. 'We've gone through hell to get here!' he snarled. 'We look as we do for we've been living rough after fighting for our lives. But know this, I am Wulfric and was chief of the guard serving Ealdorman AEthelred. I'm unarmed because I was injured in the battle and my sword was lost. Rufus here is probably the finest bowman in all Wessex and this "boy" as you call him has gifts which Alfred will surely appreciate. I'd therefore advise you not to judge us too harshly or too soon.'

With that, the third man joined us. He looked to be as broad and as strong as an ox, yet seemed more conciliatory than the others. 'Then we'd best let Alfred be the judge of that,' was all he said.

'How so?' asked Wulfric. 'Are you then part of his army?'

'No,' he laughed. 'At least, not as yet at any rate. But we will be. For word has been sent of a place where all are to assemble to await his return.'

'Where is this place?' asked Rufus.

'We'll not tell you that, for all are sworn not to make mention of it to any who are not known or who cannot be trusted. Hence men loyal to Alfred are emerging from all over the realm with just one aim – to drive Guthrum's horde out of Wessex.'

'Then can we not come with you?' asked Wulfric. 'As I said, between us we've battle skills enough to be useful.'

He thought about that for a moment. 'Very well. On the way we'll learn more about you, but if we find you've spoken falsely, we'll deal with you as we would any traitor to the Saxon cause.'

* * *

As we went, the three strangers introduced themselves. The twins were indeed brothers and were called Cedric and Cenwulf, whereas the third man was their cousin and was known as Godwin.

'So what of the invasion? Has most of Wessex yet fallen into Guthrum's hands?' I asked.

Cedric looked at me strangely. 'It's true that many people have accepted Viking rule, but others still strive to resist,' he informed us. 'We've even had word of a battle at a place called Combwich on the Parrett Estuary where the Saxons prevailed.'

'So are we going there to join them?' I pressed, realising that were walking away from Chippenham.

'No, as I told you, we're going to the place which has been set as the one where we're all to assemble. It's well away from prying eyes and Alfred will join us there and outline his plan,' explained Cedric who seemed more forthright than the others.

After several hours we stopped and made camp for the night. We allowed them a share of what remained of our provisions which seemed to set their minds at rest as to our intent.

'I'm sorry if we seemed to doubt you,' said Cedric. 'But these are dangerous times.'

'They are that,' agreed Wulfric. 'We've travelled a long way, all the time unable to be sure who could be trusted. It's no way for us to live. This was once a land where we were free to live as Saxons should.'

'And will be again, you mark my words,' offered Cedric 'There are others who, like us, are intent on taking their revenge and will give a good account of themselves, you can be sure of that!'

'Have you then fought before?' asked Wulfric.

Cedric didn't answer that which I took to mean that he hadn't. Having taken part in two battles myself and seen so many good men killed, it seemed to me that his bravado was ill placed.

'You said that young Oscar here has special gifts,' said Cedric, hurriedly changing the subject.

'That's true,' said Wulfric. 'Although I'll not say more until Alfred himself has met him.'

'Well, by tomorrow we should arrive at the place where all are to assemble. You'll no doubt meet him then.'

'Why, will he be there already?' I asked.

'I doubt it. But he'll come to join us when he can, for all the good that will do. From all we know, Guthrum can muster at least two thousand men and there's more he can call upon besides. I doubt Alfred can raise even half that number. What's more, the Vikings have spent the winter feasting and whoring whereas most of us have struggled just to survive and with barely enough food to fill our bellies.'

'You don't sound as though you think we have much chance.'

'We don't. Most of us will join Alfred knowing that to be so. But better to die in glory than to live as slaves in a divided land. Besides, what choice do we have? We must either confront Guthrum or let him conquer Wessex. Either way I doubt that many of us will live to tell the tale.'

* * *

Rufus rose early the following morning and went to hunt for more food. He returned with a brace of rabbits which he skinned and cooked for us all to eat. After that, we were ready to set off once more.

'Is the meeting place far from here?' I asked.

Cedric said that he thought it would take us most of the day to reach it, but that we could rest when we got there.

Sure enough, having travelled for several hours we came to a dense forest where there was a path which led eventually to a large clearing in which at least five hundred men had gathered, all of them armed.

'What's this place called?' I asked.

Cedric pointed to a large stone in the centre of the clearing. 'That stone is known as Egbert's Stone. It was put here by ancient hands and was once a site for pagan worship. It has since been used as a place where Saxons can meet.' Having explained that, he then went across to speak to a man who seemed to be organising things. When he returned he told us that Alfred was expected soon.

'And is this all the support he has?' asked Rufus, clearly concerned.

'No, I'm told he has some trained warriors with him as well, but he's unlikely to have much in the way of numbers. It seems most people have accepted defeat and are now intent on acknowledging Guthrum as the new ruler of Wessex.'

'A battle with the odds stacked so firmly against us won't change that,' mused Rufus. 'If that's the way of it, I'd as soon not die for nothing.'

It was Cedric who then spoke. 'Having seen our forces assembled here, you won't be allowed to leave,' he warned. 'At least, not with your head still on your shoulders. So you might as well wait with the rest of us and see what transpires.'

'Aye,' added Wulfric. 'But don't forget that Alfred has a way of inspiring men even when others think his cause is lost.'

KING ALFRED'S RETURN

During the course of the next few days, more and more men began to drift into the camp in order to join our ranks. They mostly arrived in small groups but, whilst only a few of them looked to be seasoned warriors, they were at least all armed.

Generally, all within the camp seemed settled enough as men met up with others they knew and renewed old acquaintances. We also fared well in terms of food as wild boar, deer and other game was freely available from within the forest. Despite that, there was no doubt that most of us were dreading what lay ahead.

Alfred himself arrived two days later and brought with him yet more men. At that point I made a hurried count of our numbers and estimated that there was probably well in excess of seven hundred men present. That improved our odds slightly but was still woefully short of the numbers we would need to take on Guthrum's army. What did change was that with Alfred's arrival, the mood of men who had earlier seemed despondent suddenly improved. In fact, a cheer went up as soon as he entered the camp.

I had never seen King Alfred before but he didn't look much like the great leader he was said to be. He was dressed plainly, albeit wrapped in a purple cloak secured by an elaborate silver brooch, but he wore no crown and rode on a small white horse. He raised his hand in greeting as he arrived then rode straight to the central stone and there dismounted. Two men who had come with him also dismounted and remained at his side; one of them Wulfric recognised as being Lord Ethelnorth, the most senior Ealdorman in all Wessex. Then the strangest thing happened. Alfred began to walk among us as if it was normal for the King of Wessex to mix so freely with ordinary men.

It was clear that Alfred knew some of the thanes and nobles who were with us, although probably not all of them by name. However, when he reached our small group he greeted Wulfric warmly. 'Good to have you with us,' he said. 'I'll have need of warriors like you and would have you attend me shortly.' At that he then moved on.

'Do you then know Lord Alfred?' asked Cedric, clearly impressed by the encounter.

Wulfric nodded. 'Aye. I was one of those who fought at Ashdown and he's a man who remembers those who have served him well.'

'I'm sorry, we didn't realise…'

'How could you have known given the state of us,' said Wulfric kindly.

After a while, Alfred returned to Egbert's Stone and word went round that he wanted to see all the nobles and trained warriors. A surprisingly large number of the men went forward, including Wulfric. When he returned, he explained that Alfred had yet to form a plan but would address us all later. In the meantime, he wanted to see Rufus and I.'

'Why me?' I asked.

'Lord AEthelred was Alfred's cousin, albeit a distant one, and he wants to know more about how he died. I didn't witness it myself as I was wounded at the time so I suggested he speak with you.'

We all three of us went to see him and, after waiting for a while, were well received when Wulfric introduced us. It was Rufus who explained how Lord AEthelred had died.

'Sire, there was nothing anyone could do to save him,' said Rufus. 'He insisted on leading the charge into the enemy's ranks himself and paid dearly for his courage. I regret he was slain on the field and his body was then, like others, cruelly despoiled.'

Alfred seemed to take that badly but then turned his attention to us.

'Sire, Rufus is probably one of the best bowmen in all Wessex,' said Wulfric.

Alfred smiled. 'Is that true, Rufus? Are you one of the best in all Wessex?'

'No Sire,' said Rufus.

'What, do you doubt your ability?'

'No Sire, but I'm not *one* of the best bowman. I'm *the* best bowman.'

Alfred laughed. 'And proud of it no doubt,' he said, then turned to me. 'And what about this boy? What skill does he have?'

'Sire this boy is named Oscar, son of Oswald. Although young, Lord AEthelred saw in him the ability to plan a strategy for battle which he regarded very highly.'

'Yet Lord AEthelred died in battle. Did you not advise him then?'

'I did Sire, but he declined my advice.'

'Have you then witnessed many battles, Oscar?'

'No Sire. But when discussing the tactics to be employed I seem to see things differently to others.'

'Do you, by God. Then what do you see of the battle which lies ahead of us? I'm minded to fight it at a place called Iley Oak where there's a large open heath. That should be well suited to the tactics of the shield wall which would be our best defence. What say you to that?' he pressed.

I hadn't at that point had a chance to think about it but quickly gathered my thoughts. 'Sire, if you fight on an open heath you'll surely lose,' I managed.

A gasp went up from those around us.

'How so?' demanded Alfred.

'Because Sire, being outnumbered, Guthrum's men will be able to outflank you and, in so doing, surround you. Once engulfed any chance of victory will be lost.'

Suddenly everyone was silent.

'So how do we redress that?' asked Alfred. 'Do you have any tactics in mind which might suit us better?'

'The tactic is sound, Sire. It's the location that's wrong. You need a place where there is a steep slope but where the ground on either side of it is difficult for men to tackle whilst maintaining any sort of formation.'

'I know of such a place,' said Alfred, seemingly impressed with what I'd told him. 'It's called Edington: I once went there to witness the signing of a charter. It's but an hour's march from Chippenham but how would going there help us to win?'

'Sire, if you were to occupy the ridge, Guthrum's men would be all but exhausted by the time they reach you. Also, if the terrain prevents them from spreading out, they'll not be able to engulf you.'

Alfred seemed almost speechless as he considered all I'd said. 'It would take a full day's march for such a large band of men to reach Edington,' he mused. 'We plan to spend the night at Iley Oak where others are waiting to join us but going on from there raises the risk of being seen by Guthrum's spies.'

'But they wouldn't know where we're headed, Sire. At least, not until it's too late. So long as we get to Edington before they do and secure the ridge, that's all that matters.'

Alfred acknowledged that. 'So why would Guthrum not simply ignore us?' he asked, as if testing me.

'Sire, he can't afford to. If left alive, you'll remain as a thorn in his side forever. Besides, if his intent is to conquer all Wessex he has to leave Chippenham sooner or later. He dare not do that if you are so close by that you could slip into the settlement and retake it whilst he's away. He'll therefore have no option but to fight you. We just have to make sure that when that happens, you win.'

'Where did you learn these skills?' he asked.

'I don't know Sire. I learned much about battles from my father who used to tell me stories about those in which he'd fought. I always listened intently, so perhaps that's where it comes from.'

At that he rested his hand on my shoulder. 'That being so, young Oscar, I would speak with you some more.'

* * *

Later that evening, Alfred prepared to address us all and I wondered what he could possibly say to rouse the men from all their doubts about the coming battle. Then, without any warning, he climbed up and stood on Egbert's Stone itself. As he did so, the whole camp gathered round to hear him.

'The time has come for us to avenge the Saxon blood which has been spilt so freely in this land,' he announced. 'I will not say that what lies ahead of us will be easy. Guthrum has many men to command and they are all well fed and rested if ill prepared to fight. I therefore call upon you to follow me to meet him in open battle, to retake Chippenham and then drive him and his horde back beyond the borders of my realm. I ask this as your liege and Bretwalda. Indeed, I command it as your King.'

No one spoke so Alfred continued. 'Remember, these heathens would take your daughters to be used as whores and your sons for slaves. They've already ravaged both Mercia and Northumbria, destroying homes and all that which was once part of our Saxon way. I'll not have them do the same here so what I must ask of you is this - will you stand with me and fight or have you come here to watch as they make free with all that we hold dear?'

A voice rose up from the crowd but I couldn't see who spoke. 'But Sire, if we fight them, can we win? Guthrum has many men to command who have spent a warm winter. As you've said, they're all well fed and rested.'

Alfred seemed to consider his answer very carefully. 'Those who fought beside me at Ashdown had best answer that. There we scored a resounding victory which was also very much against the odds.'

'But what if we lose?' asked another man.

Alfred shrugged. 'Then we shall die. For my part I would as soon die as a Saxon than live as a slave.'

'Perhaps,' said another voice. 'But we have fought before. And bled. And suffered. Yet still the heathens come. Wave after wave of them, Sire – more than we can count. If we fight them now, who's to say they'll not come again and in even greater numbers?'

'Not I,' answered Alfred simply. 'Yet we are Saxons. Our fathers fought for this land as did their fathers before them. Are we not the sons of those great men? Does their blood not flow within our veins?' At that, Alfred drew a small dagger. Baring his arm, he ran the blade of it across his forearm for all to see, then allowed a few drops of blood to fall onto Egbert's Stone itself. 'My line goes back beyond the memory of any man alive and deep into our history. Witness how I've spilled that pure and untainted blood here before you as it drains onto this hallowed stone. And I shall spill yet more of it if that's what it takes to drive the heathens from my realm. In fact, I would offer every drop just to see this land safe and my people restored. Thus I ask only this of you. Who will stand with me?'

The answer was a cheer which echoed through the Saxon ranks stirring even the doubtful souls to join him.

* * *

Later, as Wulfric, Rufus and I were sitting around a fire, Rufus still seemed unsure about all that was about to happen. 'Well,' he said. 'That seems to settle it. I assume you're both intent on following Alfred into battle?'

In my mind there was no doubt but that it was our duty to do so. However, before answering, I looked around and could see that the mood within the camp had definitely improved even more. Men were suddenly collecting up their things ready to follow Alfred to Iley Oak and thence to Edington where we would make our stand.

'We have no option,' replied Wulfric as if echoing my thoughts. 'Many of us will surely perish in the coming battle but we are all that's left to defend our Saxon ways and prevent this land from falling into heathen hands. It's therefore our solemn duty to go with him to defeat Guthrum - or to die trying.'

WE PREPARE FOR BATTLE

We marched out early the next morning, a long train of men following their King to battle. Looking along the line, they seemed an unlikely band for, whilst most of the trained warriors and nobles were well armed and had adequate war gear, the rest had brought whatever weapons they had. It was mostly bows or spears and such like but others had brought farming tools they'd taken from their barns or weapons they'd fashioned for themselves. Few of them had a helmet and hardly any of them had any form of mail vest.

'What's at Iley Oak?' I asked Wulfric as he, Rufus and I walked together. I was pleased to note that Wulfric seemed much restored by the prospect of being part of Alfred's comeback.

'The Oak itself is old and withered,' he told us. 'It remains an ancient meeting place but I don't expect we'll stay there long if we mean to reach Edington before Guthrum.'

Even as we marched, other men came to join our ranks and, when we got to Iley Oak, there were already others there waiting to join us as well. 'How many of us are there now, would you say?' I asked.

'Perhaps as many as a thousand all told,' replied Wulfric. 'Who would have thought that Alfred could rouse so many? It's what, barely three months since he was all but annihilated at Chippenham yet he now has a credible army at his disposal.'

As we all settled in for the night, what little food we had was shared between us and word was passed round that we should rise early in order to reach Edington before nightfall the following day. Once there, Alfred would secure the ridge but we already had word by then that Guthrum and his army were preparing to leave Chippenham.

I began to realise what that meant. We had a good force of men and Alfred had given them all the encouragement they needed to follow him, yet the question remained as to whether that would be enough to defeat such a large army, particularly one which had such a fearsome reputation.

* * *

As expected, it took us a full day to reach Edington and we arrived at dusk. There were even more men there waiting to join us, including a group of men from Mercia who had been sent by King Coelwulf as a gesture of his support. That was surprising as terms between Wessex and Mercia were often somewhat strained and King Coelwulf had already succumbed to the Vikings and now ruled only in their name. Thus several men expressed surprise at finding them there, saying that they couldn't be trusted. However, Alfred had no such reservations and dismissed their concerns. 'King Coelwulf and I have an understanding,' he assured us. 'Although unable to be here in person without arousing suspicion, he'll stand by me if I stand by him once the Vikings are defeated here.'

The men from Mercia had already established a camp on the ridge so others settled there as well, forming groups, each of them around a small fire. There was very little food to be shared but it hardly mattered as few of us felt able to eat given what we would face in the morning. Some men boasted about the battles they'd taken part in or shared memories of warriors they'd known who had died, but most of us just sat in silence as we contemplated our fate.

Alfred sent word that the senior men – ealdormen, thanes, governors and the like should all attend him. Inevitably that included Wulfric but I was surprised when Rufus and I were summoned as well. Once we'd all assembled, Alfred insisted that we gather in close, anxious that the rest of the men shouldn't hear what was discussed, for not all of it was likely to be good news and besides, he needed to be wary of spies.

'Sire, do you have a plan?' asked one man who I think was a thane of some standing.

Alfred was slow to answer. 'Let me first explain why I've chosen this place to make our stand. It stems from something suggested by young Oscar here. It seems he has some insight in such matters.'

Several of the men laughed at that.

'Trust me,' chided Alfred. 'We ignore a man's insight at our peril. In fact, I was urged to raise this army in a dream. In that dream, none other than St Cuthbert himself appeared and told me to avenge the Holy Church and assured me of success. That seemed all but impossible at the time yet here we are, ready and able to take on Guthrum's horde. So don't dismiss such things just because you don't understand them.' At that he looked around but none of the men were still laughing. 'You asked about my plan and the answer is that it's very simple. We occupy the ridge and force them to charge uphill in order to reach us. When they do, we'll drive them back all the way to Chippenham.'

'A shield wall! said one of the men, a huge barrel of a man who was clearly a warrior. 'Now that's what I call proper fighting!'

'Aye, a shield wall,' confirmed Alfred. 'But that alone won't suffice. We'll form three ranks. The first will comprise the experienced warriors in two rows, one interlocking their shields and the other standing behind them and using spears to skewer as many Vikings as they can. Behind them will stand a second rank ready to replace any who fall and thus reinforce our front line so that it's fully manned at all times. The bowmen will stand behind them both. Their task will be to loose arrows into the air to impede the Vikings as they charge up the hill towards us. After that they'll continue to shoot, trying to kill others as they retreat.'

Alfred stopped there to give us all time to consider his plan.

'Sire, from what we know, they'll greatly outnumber us,' said one man. 'What's to stop them engulfing us from either side?'

'That's why I've chosen this place,' answered Alfred. 'As you can see, the slope is steep but the terrain on either side of it is all but impossible to traverse. They'll therefore have no option but to attack us head on and won't be able to spread out and use their superior numbers to any real effect. Once we've driven them back down the slope we'll charge after them, giving them no time to regroup. The land there is level enough to become our killing ground.'

There was no doubt that everyone approved, although we all knew that the cost to both sides was likely to be high.

'Sire, where would you have us stand?' asked one of the nobles present, no doubt speaking for many of the others.

'You'll each fight beside your men,' Alfred informed him. 'They'll follow you and will be more inclined to stand with you even if things don't go well.'

'Then who will command us?'

'I will command you. I'll have runners to bring you your orders as the fight progresses. Beyond that, Lord Ethelnorth will command the first rank and Wulfric here the second. Not many of you know Wulfric but he has fought beside me before and I know him to be a good warrior.' He then looked to Rufus. 'Rufus, I would have you command the bowmen for few of them will be able to match your skill.'

'Have you then brought us here to die within the ranks!' complained one of the nobles.

'No, I would have you fight alongside your men that you might inspire them. I would have you lead them and urge them to achieve a resounding victory, for nothing less than that will suffice if I'm to restore my Kingdom.'

THE BATTLE OF EDINGTON

We began to stir the following morning even before it was light. Few of us had slept well and all had spent a cold night dreading what would surely transpire as the day unfolded.

There was no sign of Guthrum's army as we looked out onto what would become the battlefield, but all the reports we'd received confirmed that it would indeed be coming... and soon. Thus men gradually started to busy themselves sharpening blades and donning what war gear they had. All the horses had been taken to the rear the night before; all, that is, save one which belonged to a man named Dudwine who it seemed would be the only one of us mounted during the battle. When I asked Alfred why that was so, he assured me that all would become clear as the battle developed. I sensed even then that he was uneasy about what that would involve.

Some men knelt in the cold morning air and whispered prayers whilst others sat in silence, no doubt trying to summon the courage they would need for what lay ahead. To that end, several priests wandered among us giving blessings and confirming that we were not only fighting for our lives, for our land and for our King, but also for the Holy church. Then, when we least expected it, the cry went up to say that Guthrum's army had at last arrived.

As we all stood to see the enemy for the first time, we were shocked to find that there were so many of them. I tried to make a rough estimate of their numbers as I stood with Wulfric and Rufus.

'Two thousand at least,' muttered Wulfric knowing what I was itching to ask.

'That's more than two to one!' said Rufus, clearly still worried about the odds against us.

'Yes, but it's not as simple as that,' explained Wulfric. 'We're told that they're all well fed and rested but, if they've spent the winter whoring and drinking, most will be in no fit state to fight. In fact, quite a few of them will doubtless struggle just to make it up that slope in order to reach us!'

I realised then why Alfred had positioned the bowmen behind our ranks. If the Vikings did indeed struggle as they advanced towards us, they would make easy targets.

With that, Alfred himself strolled amongst us. 'They're nothing but a rabble,' he said loud enough for those closest to him to hear. 'I fear they've come looking for breakfast rather than a fight!' The jest was repeated throughout our ranks and did much to raise our spirits, particularly as we could see that the enemy had arrived in no proper order and with little in the way of discipline.

Keen to get matters underway, Alfred calmly gave the order for men to form up. 'You all know your places.' he said, then turned to Wulfric. 'Follow Lord Ethelnorth's lead,' he advised. 'He knows well enough what he's about. Apart from that, just keep your position behind your men and wait for any orders from me. Rufus, have your men hold off until the main body of their army is almost upon us then loose a volley of arrows such that they'll stagger beneath its weight. After that, have your men shoot at will but be ready to then follow behind the two front ranks if and when they advance down the slope.'

'What about me, Sire? I asked. 'Where would you have me stand?'

'With me, of course,' he said. 'We'll position ourselves to one side of the slope from where we can best watch as the battle unfolds. I shall welcome any advice you can offer but won't promise that I shall always heed it.'

* * *

Without doubt, waiting was the worst part of it, particularly once the Vikings began to form themselves into some sort of order under the respective banners of the boar, the wolf and the bear to mention but a few.

'We shouldn't underestimate them,' noted Wulfric quietly. 'They're still a force to be reckoned with but, if they intend to beat us, they'll need to fight as one; not have some factions preferring to take their lead from their own warlord or chieftain. That could work to our advantage.'

His words seemed to offer some hope but, even as he spoke, a Lur sounded out across the battlefield and the Vikings began to advance towards us as a solid mass of men.

As I'd hoped, the slope quickly proved to be their undoing. By the time they were half way up they had already become separated; some lagging behind whilst others surged forward anxious to claim their share of blood and glory. Alfred sent word to Rufus telling him to wait. Only when they were all within range did he give the signal for the bowmen to loose their arrows. They did so at once, sending a shower of them over the heads of our men and into the Viking horde.

Many Vikings cowered beneath their shields as they watched their comrades fall. Some of them managed to shoot back at us but, for the most part, their arrows landed far short of their target or were easily deflected by our shields. Rufus then ordered his men to shoot at will but, whilst effective, arrows were never going to be enough to stop the Viking advance – we all knew that only blood and dogged determination would achieve that. In fact, no sooner had the arrows exacted their toll than the Vikings hurriedly re-formed and prepared to charge up the last and steepest part of the slope, jeering and screaming their abuse.

Although our men were impatient for battle, Lord Ethelnorth ordered them to wait. Only when the Vikings were close enough did one of our number start up the Saxon battle chant of OUT! OUT! OUT! As others joined in, their voices could be heard even above the battle cries of the enemy.

'BRACE!' shouted Lord Ethelnorth as loud as he could. The men didn't need to hear, him - they all knew exactly what to do and, as the Vikings slammed into them, they took the onslaught bravely and stopped them in their tracks.

What followed can only be described as utter carnage as both sides pushed and shoved trying to gain ground. Those behind the first row of our shield wall probed any gaps with their spears, killing or maiming many. The noise was deafening as both sides hacked and slashed at each other with swords and axes and, from where I stood beside Alfred, it was impossible to say who was winning. The fighting was so fierce and the ranks packed so tightly together that some of the men who were killed couldn't even find a space in which to fall.

Wulfric had his men move closer so that they could fill any gaps in case the Vikings broke through our shield wall, whilst Rufus ensured that his bowmen kept shooting to pick off the stragglers beyond the line of those who were actually fighting. It soon became clear that the Vikings couldn't hope to hold against the slope. The turf beneath their feet was already slippery with blood and gore and they had to step over the bodies of their own comrades just to reach us. In the end they had no choice but to fall back. As they did so, our men started to follow them down the slope but Lord Ethelnorth called them back.

'We advance as one!' he ordered, then looked back at Alfred who confirmed he should proceed. At that, his rank began to advance slowly towards them, keeping their formation.

Wulfric's group followed the front rank as did the bowmen led by Rufus, but both kept their men ten or twenty paces back from those in front so they could finish off any of the wounded Vikings. I saw one who had somehow slipped past the first rank and was screaming his defiance. Either he hadn't seen Wulfric's men or perhaps he was beyond caring. Either way, he was cruelly cut down as soon as our men reached him.

The Vikings had begun to reform at the foot of the slope and, when he saw that, Lord Ethelnorth didn't hurry but simply continued to march doggedly towards them. Alfred quickly relayed orders to Wulfric, telling him to have his men merge with those of Lord Ethelnorth's - which they did, spreading out to fill any gaps where men had fallen or to relieve the wounded. Once joined, Lord Ethelnorth gave the order to attack.

'CHARGE!' he bellowed, and the combined ranks smashed into the Vikings, hitting them like a hammer.

What followed was like nothing I'd ever seen. The shield walls had somehow dissolved and the battle became a melee of men fighting for all they were worth, slicing and jabbing with whatever weapons they had, hacking each other down. The noise was terrifying as men screamed in pain or from the madness which they seemed to find in war. Once again, from where we were it was all but impossible to see who was having the best of it, but Alfred had yet another ruse to play. He signalled for Dudwine to join us. 'Go when you will,' he said quietly, as though it was an order he was reluctant to give.

'Go where?' I asked, still having no idea what Alfred had in mind.

'I'm to seize their Raven Banner,' explained Dudwine proudly.

I looked at him, almost incredulous. 'They'll tear you apart for that!' I warned.

'Aye, but if I try, Alfred has promised to restore my uncle's lands to our family. They were forfeit to him when my uncle refused to support him and I must recover them if I can, if only for the sake of my son.'

'I'm sure your son would rather have his father than his uncle's lands,' I replied.

But Dudwine clearly didn't see it that way. 'Without lands we're nothing,' he reasoned then, loyally bowing his head to his King, he rode proudly down the slope.

We both watched as our men parted to allow Dudwine through. He then scythed his way into the midst of the enemy ranks, slashing with his sword as he went. All I can say is that he was the bravest man I'd ever seen. He hacked with his sword at anyone who tried to stop him, turning this way and that, killing any in his path as he did so. Then, when he was close enough, he hurled his sword at one of the Vikings and, having thus freed his hand, reached out to grasp the very tip of their sacred banner. The man who held it wouldn't let go at first but, when Dudwine spurred his horse, he had no choice but to release it. Even though he then had the banner, Dudwine had so many men pressed about him that he couldn't turn his horse in order to ride back to the relative safety of our ranks. All he could do was to hurl the banner back to one of our men who, as he received it, held it aloft as almost every Saxon in the field cheered.

Seeing what was afoot, Rufus moved to where he could offer Dudwine support by picking off some of those who were trying to stop him. But, having being unable to carry a shield whilst riding and using a sword at the same time, Dudwine had nothing with which to protect himself. Thus his fate was sealed as he took blow after blow before falling from his horse and disappearing into a sea of very angry men.

The loss of their sacred Raven Banner was certainly the turning point of the battle and with it, Guthrum's men lost heart. They began to hurriedly retreat from the field as a disorderly rabble.

'Follow them!' ordered Lord Ethelnorth when he realised they were beaten. 'Don't let them find the safety of the Vill at Chippenham!' Our men were only too happy to oblige, killing the wounded and stripping what they could from the dead and the dying. 'Don't waste your time on trinkets!' he urged. 'There's plunder enough for us all!'

One group of about a dozen Vikings threw down their weapons to surrender but Lord Ethelnorth was having none of it. 'Put them to the sword,' he ordered. 'Kill them and have done with it.'

The men did as he ordered.

Under the close protection of his personal guard, Alfred and I had, by that time, made our way down the slope. As we went, we found it littered with dead and dying men, not to mention discarded weapons and war gear. When we reached the rest of our men, I was relieved to find that both Wulfric and Rufus had survived the fray, although when I spoke to Godwin, he sadly informed me that both Cedric and Cenwulf had been slain.

Meanwhile, Lord Ethelnorth kept urging everyone to keep following the Vikings as they retreated.

'Do as he says,' ordered Alfred. 'If we don't stop them now they'll take refuge in the Vill and it'll then be the devil's own job to shift them.'

They were both right. By the time we reached Chippenham, Guthrum and what was left of his army were indeed safely back inside the Vill and had closed the gates against us.

THE PRICE OF PEACE

Alfred summoned all the senior Saxons just as he had done before the battle. As they gathered around him, he outlined his plan to oust the Vikings from the Vill. 'We need to achieve a complete victory here if the Saxon people are to support me,' he said. 'Thus we cannot allow Guthrum and his horde to slip away only to fight us again. Post men at various points and bring to me any of the Vikings who are caught trying to escape from the Vill.'

'Sire, what will you do with them?' asked one man.

'I'll have them put to the sword in full view of their comrades. That should deter others from trying to escape.'

'But surely, if they slip away my Lord, would that not suit us better?' suggested Lord Ethelnorth, nursing a wound to his arm.

'No,' said Alfred firmly. 'They won't have prepared for a siege so I would have as many of them as possible stay within the Vill. The more mouths they have to feed the sooner they'll surrender. In the meantime, keep your men busy. They'll all want to return to their homes with whatever spoil they've taken and I can't afford for them to leave as yet. Attend to our wounded and, to keep the men busy, have them start to dig graves for those of us who have fallen and place all the bodies of the Vikings on a pile over there ready for burning.'

'Sire, our men will have farms which they've neglected and crops to sow,' suggested one man.

'Exactly. So remind them that my Hall in Chippenham will be stock full of whatever's been looted and there'll be a share for all. They'll not want to miss out on that!'

* * *

Word was sent to Guthrum entreating him to surrender but it was over a week before the gates were finally opened and a band of a dozen warriors rode out. Alfred recognised Guthrum at once and, as several of his personal guard stepped forward with their swords drawn ready to protect him, he greeted the Viking leader and his jarls, though not in their language.

'I thought you could speak their tongue,' whispered Lord Ethelnorth.

'I can,' said Alfred. 'But sometimes it's better to negotiate when they don't know that you understand what they say to each other. Besides, they'll have brought an interpreter.'

With that, a man rode forward and dismounted. He was old and walked with a limp but seemed to speak our tongue well enough. 'Lord Guthrum is wishing for peace,' he said, bowing respectfully. 'If you will have it so.'

Alfred indicated that Guthrum should also dismount and step forward but that the remaining members of his party were to remain where they were.

Guthrum was a giant of a man, swathed in furs and with a thick black beard and hair which was braided with silver bands. He said nothing, preferring to leave his interpreter to speak on his behalf instead.

'I am Ulf,' said the interpreter. 'You I assume are Lord Alfred for whom we are with much respect. We know you to be a brave and valiant warrior and a wise king.'

Alfred acknowledged the compliment but didn't respond in kind as was expected. Ulf then made an aside to Guthrum.

'He said we're discourteous dogs,' whispered Alfred, anxious not to show that he'd understood what was said between them. He then returned his attention to Ulf. 'Tell Lord Guthrum that I call upon him to surrender,' he said aloud. 'I require him and his men to hand over their weapons and offer back the Vill at Chippenham with all booty intact. Also, all Saxons taken as slaves and held there shall be freed and given to our care.'

As this was repeated to Guthrum he feigned surprise.

'I've not come to negotiate,' snapped Alfred. 'You're beaten and will accept what's offered. It's that or starve.' With that he turned as if to walk away.

'Lord Guthrum asks you to spare the lives of his men,' said Ulf.

'Does he then offer them as slaves?' asked Alfred.

Ulf quickly conferred with Guthrum. 'No, my Lord. He demands that they leave as free men.'

'He's beaten and can demand nothing!' stormed Alfred. 'If they prefer they can join their fallen comrades on the funeral pyre. I offer them an honourable death, nothing more.'

Guthrum had clearly expected no quarter and seemed resigned to that, knowing that most of his men would prefer death to either of the other two options - slavery or starvation.

Alfred then seemed to have further thoughts. 'I am conscious that there has been enough blood spilt in this land,' he said. 'As a Christian, I'm minded to spare your men if they surrender their weapons and depart this land in peace. However, the lives of Guthrum and all his Jarls of senior rank shall be forfeit.'

The proposal was hurriedly explained to Guthrum who seemed unperturbed by it.

'My Lord Guthrum says that he will offer his life but no other,' said Ulf.

At that, Alfred stepped forward and, taking Guthrum by the elbow, led him aside so they could speak in private. To everyone's surprise, he did so in the Danish tongue. It was some time before they both returned.

'Guthrum has agreed to accept baptism,' announced Alfred. 'He and twelve senior Jarls shall take instruction in our faith and I shall stand sponsor for them at the font. On that basis, the lives of all his men who convert to Christianity shall be spared.'

There was a hushed silence as we all of us took that in.

'But Sire, what then?' asked one man.

'After that Guthrum shall take lands which he may govern in my name. He's free to distribute these to those of his men who wish to live in peace. The rest must depart this land and swear never to return to Wessex.'

'Why have we fought so hard to take back lands from these heathens only to give them back to the very people who took them from us in the first place!' complained Lord Ethelnorth, loudly voicing what many of us were thinking.

'Because we are few and they are many, that's why,' explained Alfred. 'They came here in search of land, not blood. If we give them the means to support themselves and their families, they'll have no cause to rise up against us. It's better that we rule by consent rather than force. Besides, we've already paid a high price for trying to hold back this invasion. Now it's time to try a new way in the hope that it will lead to peace.'

* * *

As negotiations to finalise the treaty got under way, Guthrum's men came out and formed a line, tossing their weapons and war gear onto a pile then standing ready to accept their mass conversion to Christianity. There was no formal instruction in our faith and we all knew that it would lack any substantial root, but a priest went along the line making the sign of the cross as he went. Those who refused to kneel and kiss his crucifix as a sign that they accepted their new God were put to the sword there and then and their bodies were added to the pile of Vikings who had been killed in the battle itself.

Whilst this was going on, Rufus took a few of us hunting for deer or boar which would be needed for a feast we had planned to mark Alfred's great triumph. We were warned to take great care as there were still groups of disgruntled Vikings who had fled the field of battle and not retreated with the others to Chippenham. They therefore remained armed and were no doubt intent on vengeance.

Having led us through a forest, Rufus managed to bring down a deer and was busy examining the kill whilst I was standing beside him. We neither of us saw the man who, from the cover of a tree, loosed a single arrow. Whilst presumably intended for Rufus, it was not a skilled shot, for it missed its mark but instead lodged deep into my thigh. As it did so, I cried out in pain then slumped forward before falling to lay face down on the ground.

Rufus and the others were quick to attend me. They turned me over and covered me with a cloak but Rufus stopped them from trying to withdraw the arrow. 'If you do we'll not be able to stop the bleeding,' I heard him say. With that they carried me back to our camp.

* * *

I recall very little of what followed. I do remember being given something to drink which I was told would ease my pain although, for the most part, I was left to manage that for myself. As I did so, I seemed to drift in and out of consciousness but I do know that, at some point, Alfred himself came to see me, although what was said was somehow lost in the shadows of my mind. After that I was taken to a nunnery just outside Chippenham where it was thought the nuns would have some skill in dealing with injuries such as mine. Once again, I remember nothing of the journey itself except that I was carried on a litter by two men with others keeping guard the whole way – something which had been ordered by none other than Alfred himself.

When we eventually reached the nunnery, I was taken into a small chamber and was made to drink from a bowl which contained some potion which I was told would make me sleep. Sure enough, some time then passed before I eventually awoke to find myself being tended by a young woman who, strange to say, was not dressed in the habit of a nun. She seemed vaguely familiar but, being newly conscious, I couldn't quite place her. At that point, I was concerned to find myself lying on a cot, stripped naked as she gently washed my body, seemingly unashamed at seeing me in that state. I tried to look down at my leg but couldn't see the wound itself as it had been tightly bandaged.

'Did the arrow come out cleanly?' I asked as she stood with her back to me, rinsing out the blood from the cloth she'd used to wash me. It was only as she turned to answer that my heart soared as I realised who she was.

'Edwina!' I said. 'Is it really you?'

She blushed and came across to stand beside me. As she did so, I hurriedly tried to cover myself as best I could.

'But I thought you dead!' I said, recalling that she had remained at the Vill once her father had been killed and all our men had either retreated or been slain.

'There have been many times when I've wished I had been killed,' she said quietly.

'Well, you're safe enough now,' I managed. 'How did you manage to escape from the Vill?'

She was silent for a moment. 'I didn't,' she said bitterly. 'I was taken by the Vikings and passed between them like so much baggage. I was beaten and ill used by at least a dozen of them until they brought me here when they came to join Guthrum. I pray only that they all died in the battle and suffered dreadfully for what they did to me.'

'So how did you get free of them?' I asked.

She meekly bowed her head. 'I will never be free of them,' she said. 'For I have to live with the shame of having been abused by so many men. But, as they left to fight Alfred, I was at least able to slip away.'

I could find no words to console her, so said nothing.

'I've thought many times about killing myself, but feared that I might be with child,' she continued. 'If so, it would be a sin to take my own life as I would be taking that of the unborn child's as well.'

'So what will you do?' I asked.

She shrugged. 'The good sisters here have taken me in and have offered me shelter. If I am with child they'll decide what's best to be done. If it's a girl she will no doubt remain here to be raised as a member of their order but if it's a boy…'

'Surely a boy can be given out for adoption?'

She shook her head. 'He'll be the bastard son of a Viking and, as such, no one will want to take him in lest he carries the bad blood of his father in his veins.'

I could see her plight but could think of nothing to console her.

'And what of you?' she asked. 'How will you now manage?'

'Hopefully, once my leg has healed I'll be able to resume my duties. Alfred has asked to see me so hopefully he'll offer me a position and….'

Even as I spoke, I realised she was looking at me somewhat sadly. 'I regret that your leg will never heal,' she said softly.

'Why? Surely having removed the arrow it will mend soon enough?'

'The arrow was too deep set. It was barbed so they couldn't just withdraw it. Instead they had no choice but to push it through and, in so doing, the shaft splintered. All they could do was to cut into the flesh more deeply until they found the splinters, but that caused much damage to be done. They say that you will never walk again except with a crutch to support you.'

* * *

I remained at the nunnery for several days before Wulfric came to visit me. 'How's the wound?' he asked.

'It seems that I'll never walk again unaided,' I said, trying not to sound too morose even though I was still in pain. 'Are things now settled between Alfred and Guthrum?' I asked, changing the subject.

'Aye, it seems there is now a measure of agreement between them, but the terms are still to be finalised. It seems that Guthrum will rule some lands beyond Wessex but in Alfred's name. In the meantime, there's much to be done to restore things. Our land has been ravaged with many homes and farmsteads pillaged and destroyed, all of which needs to be set to rights. Besides, small bands of Vikings are still raiding freely where they will.'

'And what of you and Rufus? Are you both well?'

He confirmed that they were and told me that Alfred had again asked after me. 'He would have you attend him when you're well enough,' he said. 'But I told him you must first return to see your parents who know only that you've been wounded. I'll take you there if you're well enough to travel.'

'Thank you, but I'm sure you have other things to attend to and I wouldn't wish to take you out of your way.'

He nodded as if to acknowledge that. 'That's true enough,' he agreed. 'But the things I have to attend to are all at Lord AEthelred's Vill. As you'll recall, the settlement was ransacked and many parts of it were destroyed completely. The people are gradually returning to repair their homes and I am to administer matters as a temporary Ealdorman until a new man can be appointed. I've asked Rufus to join me and would have you do the same once you're well.'

I hardly needed to be asked and would have accepted at once but for the wound to my leg. Wulfric dismissed that and joked that if I was unable to walk, he'd find a man to carry me on his back if that would help. It was then that I mentioned Edwina. 'May I bring her with me to live at the Vill?' I asked.

He was more than a little surprised at that. 'You are aware of her predicament?' he asked. 'She's been abused by more men than she can count and may even be with child.'

I thought carefully before I said anything which I might later regret. 'She carries no shame for that so far as I'm concerned,' I said. 'She is of such a gentle nature and the Vill was once her home, so I would wish to see her taken in and her reputation thereby restored so far as that can be managed.'

'Yes, but who in their right mind would take her to wife and regard any child she carries as his own?' he asked

Again I was slow to answer. 'I would,' I managed at last. 'If she would have me.'

Wulfric looked shocked and was almost lost for words, but he could see I was serious. 'Then on your head be it,' was all he said.

* * *

Edwina wept when I asked her to marry me. She was at pains to be sure that I fully understood about all that which she had been forced to endure but, when I told her that I didn't care about that, we embraced. Strangely, it was the first time I'd ever held her or indeed any woman but, as I did so, I knew that somehow things would be right between us.

Wulfric and Rufus returned a few days after that and I need hardly say that I was pleased to see them both. They brought a small cart with them for me to travel in as they knew I would be unable to ride with my leg as it was. Edwina seemed shy when I explained to Rufus that she and I were to wed and that she would therefore be travelling with us. He said nothing, but I could tell that neither he nor Wulfric truly approved. Nonetheless, we journeyed together from there to visit my father and mother.

* * *

When we at last arrived at my parent's farmstead, my father and mother both came out to greet me, surprised to see me having received no word of my coming. I was determined not to let my father see me as a cripple, so insisted on walking the last few steps, albeit I needed Rufus to support me.

As my father embraced me, both he and my mother were anxious to know about the extent of my wound, but were proud when I told them that I had actually met King Alfred and that he had personally asked to see me.

'And who is this young lady?' asked my father, looking at Edwina.

'Father, do you not recognise her?' I asked. 'This is Edwina, Lord AEthelred's daughter.' Even as I said it I could see what my father was thinking. The girl before him looked nothing like the bright and gay young maiden he had known. All she had suffered was somehow etched into her whole demeanour.

'And are you then retuning her to her father's Vill?' he asked.

'No father, she's returning to be my wife.'

He looked aghast as I said it, knowing full well what she would have endured. 'You do realise what you're saying?' he pressed. 'God knows how many men she's lain with. Worse still, can you be certain that she's not with child?' With that he looked her up and down as if checking for any outward sign of that.

'Yes father. I'm prepared for that.'

My father shook his head. 'You'd rear the son of another man? Even knowing what he was?'

'She's not wanton, if that's what you mean,' I argued.

'No, but surely you cannot be planning to wed a girl who carries the bastard spawn of a wretched heathen – and a Viking to boot! If you take her to wed on that basis then you're more of a fool than I took you for!'

'So, what would you have me do? I've loved her since first I saw her. She would normally have been so far above me that marriage would have been unthinkable. What's more, if she is with child and I don't wed her, that child will be killed if it's a boy or confined to a nunnery if it's a girl.'

'Yes, but neither she nor the child are any concern of yours.'

'I know as much, father. But it's not the child's fault if it's to be born from such circumstances. I'll therefore wed Edwina and rear her child if necessary. After all, what have I to offer her now that I'm virtually a cripple?'

'What? Are you hoping that she'll inherit all her late father's wealth? If so son, you'll soon be disappointed, for all he owned was taken when the Vill was ransacked.'

'I'm well set in that respect, for Wulfric has kindly offered me a position at the Vill,' I assured him.

My father seemed puzzled by that. 'And for how long will that last given that you can barely walk a step without using a stick? Without his help you'd have no way of earning a living so will be forced to then beg just to feed yourself and your dependents.'

'If that were to happen, I'd go to see Lord Alfred who would surely see me right.' Even as I said it, I knew there would be no way of persuading my father to accept what I was doing. 'I know you'll not support me in this,' I pressed. 'But if I've learned anything whilst I've been away it's that I must live to please myself, not to appease the views of others.'

* * *

Wulfric, Rufus and I were intending to return to the Vill, none of us knowing what we would find there. All we'd heard thus far was that it had been looted and all but destroyed.

As we prepared to leave, my mother wept openly whilst my father looked to be as stern as I'd ever seen him. I had hoped that with all I'd achieved he might have softened in some way but, by my being resolute, it seemed that was not to be.

Wulfric reached out and grasped my father's hand as we left, then spoke to him consolingly, but my father still seemed adamant that he could never condone my plan to wed Edwina. 'I had a dream when Oscar was first born,' he said mournfully. 'In that dream, I saw him cruelly slain whilst serving in the fyrd and I swore to ensure that fate would be avoided. Yet I never once considered that he would live to shame us in this way.'

'Yet you should be proud of him,' said Wulfric. 'He's done well by you in serving King Alfred with distinction.'

'Perhaps, but in many ways I would have preferred that he'd fallen in battle and thus died a hero,' said my father. 'At least then we could grieve for him with honour and pride, whereas now we'll have to endure the shame of having him marry a girl who has known more men that a common whore.'

'I see no shame in that,' said Wulfric. 'Of course, he could have chosen more wisely, but there are many women in this realm who have suffered in much the same way as Edwina. Yet she has borne her predicament well and for that she is to be admired. As to your son, there is much about him which reminds me of you.'

'In what way?'

Wulfric smiled. 'As I recall you were once young and reckless. For instance, that day when you saved my life - all the other men had retreated but you rode back towards the advancing enemy to save me. But for you, I would have surely been slain.'

'Pah!' said my father.

'You can dismiss what I say if you like, but I recall that after that you were offered the chance to become head of Lord AEthelred's guard before I was, but you refused it. Instead, you turned your back on your life as a much respected warrior and took to farming instead. You had the courage to follow your heart.'

'I'd had my fill of fighting,' said my father.

'Exactly my point. You knew your own mind and no man could ever have swayed you from whatever course you chose to follow. I see that Oscar is made in that same mould.'

'Yes, but what has he to gain from marrying this girl?'

'Well, for one thing he loves her. He also loves you and has looked up to you all his life. What's more, whilst I think he learned much during his recent exploits, there was one thing in particular which was important to him.'

'What was that?' asked my father.

'To prove to himself that he deserves to be called his father's son.'

THE END

GLOSSARY

Whilst not all universally accepted, the following is an explanation of some terms as used in this story:-

BRETWALDA	A mainly honorary title given to a recognised overlord
CEORL	The lowest rank of freeman
EALDORMAN	A high ranking nobleman usually appointed by the King to oversee a Shire
FYRD	A group of able-bodied freemen who could be mobilised for military service when required
JARL	A Viking nobleman or chieftain
REEVE	An official appointed to oversee specific duties. These included administrative and sometimes judicial responsibilities
SEAX	A short single edged sword
THANE	A freeman holding land granted by the King or by an Ealdorman to whom he owed allegiance and for whom he provided military support when needed
VILL	The home of a nobleman which included a large Hall, accommodation and stables etc. They were often fortified so as to form a place of refuge in the event of an attack

THE WITAN   The King's council made up of senior nobles and clergy. It advised on all important matters, particularly the appointment of a new king

AUTHOR'S NOTES

One of the many challenges facing anyone writing a book set in the so called "Dark Ages" is that there are few reliable facts to rely on and even fewer unbiased contemporary accounts of what took place. The mist surrounding the events I've described thickens considerably where intervening generations have added embellishments of their own – as is certainly the case with such an iconic personage as Alfred the Great.

That said, I never set out to write a history book as such, rather I've tried to balance "fact" and "fiction" whilst not losing sight of the need to tell a good story. That's a difficult path to tread as a writer and I therefore make no apology for my interpretation of events, even though some of the things I've described are open to debate. For example, I suggested in my first book, **Blood and Destiny,** that the Saxons may have been betrayed by someone who opened the gates to Alfred's Vill at Chippenham when it was attacked by Guthrum. There is no firm evidence for this but I question how such an accomplished and battle-hardened commander as Alfred could be taken by surprise after being at war for so long. Surely, in such troubled times, he would have posted lookouts to warn him of an approaching army? Was this just a lapse of judgement by a war weary king or were there more sinister forces at work? It's likely that many of his men would have returned to their homes and families for Christmas so he may have been woefully short-handed but, even so, it would have been difficult to breach his defences. So, was there an act of treachery, perhaps for monetary gain or, as I've implied in this book, was there a political coup by nobles who were by then tired of war?

Similarly, my description of the battle at Edington is lifted almost entirely from my own depiction of it in **Blood and Destiny** and, contentious or not, I saw no reason to change that. After all, we know very little about the battle – how many men were involved, what tactics were employed or even where it was actually fought. What I did change was to credit King Ceolwulf of Mercia with having played some part in the victory. There is certainly some evidence to support that although, once again, details are scarce.

It almost goes without saying that most of the characters in my story are fictitious, with the notable exception of Alfred himself about whom we do at least have some detailed knowledge. Based on that, I elected to portray him as a wise and benevolent King and I hope that in doing so I've done him justice.

Given that the events I've described took place over 1000 years ago, there are doubtless errors and inaccuracies in my account for which I apologise. Hopefully I have managed to capture something of the "flavour" of the period but nonetheless, this book must sit on the fiction shelf of the bookcase rather than alongside the weightier tomes written by the many eminent historians whose work I have read and enjoyed but had not the wit nor inclination to emulate.

I do hope you've enjoyed the story.

CJB

ACKNOWLEDGEMENTS

There are many people I need to thank for their contribution to this book, not least of which is my wife who has always encouraged me to continue writing even when I was tempted to stop. She has also been responsible for checking my work prior to submission, clearing up all the typos and spelling mistakes. It never ceases to amaze me how many times I can read something and fail to notice errors which should have been all too obvious!

Inevitably, as with any work of historical fiction, research has been important and I have enjoyed that aspect immensely. There are too many people who have helped with that to thank them all individually but they will know who they are. In particular, I have enjoyed meeting so many people at the various talks, book clubs and writers' groups I've attended and am very grateful to them for the insight, information and feedback they've provided.

Finally, as ever, I am grateful to my readers. Without them, writing a book would be an almost pointless exercise and I much value their support and interest in my work.

CJB

ABOUT THE AUTHOR

Chris Bishop was born in London in 1951. After a successful career as a Chartered Surveyor, he retired to concentrate on writing, combining this with his lifelong interest in Anglo Saxon history. His first novel, **Blood and Destiny**, was published in 2017 and his second, **The Warrior with the Pierced Heart**, in 2018 followed by **The Final Reckoning** in 2019 and **Bloodlines** in 2020. Together they form a series entitled **The Shadow of the Raven,** the fifth and final part of which - **The Prodigal Son** – was published in 2023.

Chris has also published numerous blogs about his work, including:-

1.   Alfred and the Vikings – a five part series:-

      a.   Alfred's troubled realm

      b.   So, who were the dreaded Vikings?

      c.   Why did the Vikings first invade England?

      d.   The (almost) forgotten battle

      e.   The ways of war at the time of King Alfred

2.   Warhorses – the use of horses in battle at the time of King Alfred the Great

3.   Wareham's past as a Saxon stronghold

4.   Was King Alfred really the father of the English Navy?

5.   So, did Alfred really burn the cakes?

These can all be viewed on his website -
www.chrisbishopauthor.com

Chris is a member of the Historical Writers' Association

You can also follow him on Twitter @CBishop_author

His other interests include travel, windsurfing and fly fishing.

Visit Chris's Historium Press page at
www.historiumpress.com/chris-bishop

or his author website at www.chrisbishopauthor.com

www.historiumpress.com